tral
vith
ment Z was
enough to sign his own death warrant. Then shortly afterwards there was an assassination in an obscure European principality. There were other deaths, until finally the British Foreign Secretary was shot down in his own office.

What was the connection between the crimes? Gradually pieced together; the outline of a fantastic plot. A trade war, a revolution, probable hot war between Russia and Germany. And all for the personal profit of a few men. Men who must be identified and destroyed by Department Z.

Also in Arrow Books by John Creasey

Carriers of Death
The Children of Despair
The Day of Disaster
Days of Danger
Dark Peril
Death by Night
Death in the Rising Sun
Death round the Corner
Dead or Alive
Island of Peril
The League of Dark Men
No Darker Crime
Panic
Redhead
Sabotage
Seven Times Seven
Shadow of Doom
The Terror Trap
Thunder in Europe

John Creasey

Menace

ARROW BOOKS

ARROW BOOKS LTD
178–202 Great Portland Street, London W1

AN IMPRINT OF THE HUTCHINSON GROUP

London Melbourne Sydney
Auckland Johannesburg Cape Town
and agencies throughout the world

*

First published by John Long Ltd 1939
First paperback edition 1941
This revised Arrow edition 1971

Made and printed in Great Britain by
Hunt Barnard Printing Ltd, Aylesbury, Bucks

ISBN 0 09 004180 1

Chapter 1

Strange Visitor

Bob Kerr had every reason in the world not to want a visitor that afternoon. The sun was shining on Brook Street with unusual brilliance, moreover he was wholly wrapt up in the prospect of an afternoon drive as far as Dorking, and then a little off the beaten track to a certain Rose Cottage. Warm August rains had prepared a splendid September, where fields of corn as yet ungathered would remind Kerr – who was listed as Number Two on the records of a peculiar Department at Whitehall, called Z – that there could be peace and serenity and freedom from the continual fear that one day a fleet of hostile aircraft would blast the quiet of the countryside into chaos.

To that aim Robert McMillan Kerr, to give him his full name, was dedicated.

On this fair afternoon with so desirable a jaunt in prospect, the world seemed bright enough. Lightened, of course, by the fact that in five minutes Lois Dacre – Number Eleven in that same Department, and also off duty – was due to call at 77g Brook Street. They were going to make an oft-promised and much delayed call on a man named Burke and the lovely Patricia, his wife.

Kerr, looking out of the window towards the Piccadilly end from which Lois would come, rubbed his chin reflectively.

And then an odd thing happened.

Kerr's lips parted in an unexpected smile. It altered the whole cast of his countenance. He hardly looked the same man.

On the opposite side of the road a man was walking. That

in itself was hardly novel enough to make Kerr smile. It was the manner of the walk; moreover the walker affected a large brown fur coat and vivid yellowish suede shoes. He was, not unnaturally, perspiring and mopping at his brow with a brightly coloured handkerchief; as far as Kerr could see his face held an expression of surprise, as though he hardly expected to be hot in an enveloping fur coat during a warm September afternoon.

Was he a foreigner or a freak?

'Odd cuss,' said Kerr to no one in particular. 'I – *blast* the thing!'

It was the telephone, strident, insistent. The room was one of three that comprised the flat, and the telephone was only answered by Mold – Kerr's man – when Kerr was absent.

Both were recent acquisitions. Mold had come from a Domestic Servants' Agency with excellent references, and Department Z had looked him over with satisfactory results. The flat he had been allowed to select without approval from Department Z.

Kerr picked up the receiver with a sigh. There was one thing he could never entirely approve in working for Z; you had to be on the *qui vive* all the time. But Kerr supposed he could hardly expect to work for the most exclusive branch of British Intelligence, and live a carefree inconsequential life as well.

But if this call was from Craigie – Craigie, the head and sinews of Department Z!

It was from Craigie; his voice, quiet and well-modulated, came all too clearly to Kerr's ears.

'No,' said Kerr, 'it's too bad. I'm positively full up for the afternoon and evening, old man, find one of the other mugs to take this job.'

Craigie chuckled.

'All right, Bob, it's not urgent. But slip over and see me sometime before midnight, will you?'

'Right. Anything big?'

'I don't know. I've had several reports in from AKA, and

I've a feeling you'll have to go over there for a bit. But it might be a false alarm. I'm waiting for confirmation. Seen Lois lately?'

'I hope to see her in about thirty seconds. Ah – here she is. 'Bye!'

He gave Gordon Craigie no opportunity for prolonging the conversation, thought fleetingly of AKA – the Department code-word for that nest of trouble in mid-Europe, the principality of Vallena – and stepped towards the door. Someone had tapped, and that someone could only be Lois.

Mold stood there, holding a visiting card before him.

'This gentleman, sir, says that he would like to see you urgently. He seems very worried, sir.'

Kerr frowned and took the card.

'Hmm. Show him in, and ask Miss Dacre to wait for a few minutes if she arrives before I'm through.'

'Very good, sir.' Mold closed the door, and Kerr walked back to the window, still holding the card. He had managed to push all thought of Lois Dacre to the back of his mind, for this was a queer business. Coincidence? Well it might be, but Kerr was inclined to look for the obvious in all things, and he wondered where he would find it here.

For the card read:

M. Jules Doriennet
Importer – Exporter
15, Maustrasse,
Baj – Vallena.

In short, Craigie had just said that Kerr might be wanted to make a trip to Vallena, and here was a native, presumably, of the country, and certainly a resident of Baj, the capital, about to enter the room.

The door opened, and Mold's impersonal voice announced 'Mr. Doriennet.' Kerr took a half step forward, and then paused imperceptibly. For here was the fur-coated pedestrian, looking even hotter at close quarters than he had done at a distance. He regarded Kerr with a pair of piercingly blue eyes.

'Ah – Mr Doriennet.' Kerr extended a hand. Doriennet's clasp was firm enough, as was to be expected, but over-warm.

'Mistah – Kerr?'

Kerr wondered why Mold had not relieved the visitor of the monstrous coat.

'That's right. Can I take your coat?'

'Thank you – no.' Doriennet hugged the fur closer to him. 'It is ver' warm, yes. No?' The expression of perpetual inquiry was surely too good to be false.

'A drink, Mr Doriennet? Whisky – beer – an iced lager?'

'Iced – lager!' Away went the expression of inquiry, to be replaced by one of pleased anticipation. Doriennet obviously took to Robert McMillan Kerr as a man after his own heart. 'Most excellent, Mistah – Kerr. My thanks.'

Kerr pressed the bell, and Doriennet sat in silence, sometimes eyeing Kerr and sometimes looking out of the window, until the drinks arrived.

"Ah-ah.' Up went the glass, and down again after a long, appreciative draught. 'So that is possible – even in England. They told me it was always so ver' cold, Mistah – Kerr.'

Kerr noticed two things. First, that his visitor always paused before uttering his name, as though he was a little uncertain whether he had contacted the right man; second, that Doriennet was suggesting this was his first visit to England, although he spoke English remarkably well with an accent of the kind that could be easily assumed.

'A judgment on us for always grumbling,' said Kerr, smiling, 'though we're very well satisfied with our climate.'

He offered cigarettes, but Doriennet preferred to smoke his own brand. Kerr waited, showing no signs of impatience. Here was a man out of the ordinary, and his call might have a rare importance.

'A mistake, yes, I understand.' Doriennet waved a forgiving hand. 'I make them, you make them, but I hope ver' much, Mistah – Kerr, I make no mistake in coming to see you.'

'So do I,' murmured Kerr.

Doriennet tapped his ash, then went on slowly: 'You are surprised at my coming, yes?'

'I try never to be surprised,' said Kerr with his widest smile. 'I've no doubt you wanted to see me.'

Doriennet nodded.

'That is so. On most important business, Mistah Kerr. My coat – you see heem?'

'I've been admiring it,' lied Kerr cheerfully.

'So. An' you think I beeg fool, yes, for leaving heem on. Don't tell me! Well, that is perhaps. In heem, Mistah Kerr, is all I have. My business – it is broke. Finished!' Doriennet waved his hands excitedly, yet he spoke with the utmost gloom and seriousness. 'It is ended, I tell you. I, Jules Doriennet, have now only enough to live. An' I carry it wit' me, Mistah Kerr – otherwise they would rob me also of that. Oh, oh, I know them and their ways. I know them – and you, you will fight them!'

Kerr was beginning to be interested.

Gone was all thought of Rose Cottage, the Burkes, Lois Dacre and an afternoon of lazy enjoyment.

'I see,' he said gravely.

'Good! I expect that, from what I have heard of you. He is the man, they say, who will act. He wastes no words. I have heard that with my own ears. You are the man I want, Mistah Kerr. I tell you I am broke – finish – done down. I, who was the most famous trader in Baj. It ees a crime, but it cannot now be prevent. It has happened, and why? Because I, Mistah Kerr, would not join them. Because I have always enjoyed working and trading with the English. They are fair, yes. They are perhaps at times the fool, but who ees not? And here am I, Mistah Kerr, a poor man with only the mon-ee I stand in, telling you this. I am ended because I am a friend of the English, and I will do no things *they* would have me do.'

Doriennet mopped his brow, drank deeply, then hitched his chair a foot nearer Kerr.

'So?'

'Who are "they"?' asked Kerr mildly.

'They are the villains!' exclaimed Doriennet with sudden wild abandon. 'They are the rogues, the devils, they would – but I am past myself! Mistah Kerr, I tell you this. I come to you because they say: "Kerr, he ees the biggest, the best man in England, for the espionage. He is clevaire, he sticks on, he is much prized by Gord-*on* Craigie'. This I hear them say when I am in a room next door. They do not think I hear, oh no. And then I hear also, they will kill me. I, Jules Doriennet, do not wish yet to die. I wish to live. And they say also this: "If we kill Kerr, then the trouble is not great". And I think, if they would kill Kerr and me, then if Kerr is told, he will work to save himself. An' then he will also help me, not to save me for I am saving myself, Mistah Kerr, but to defeat them. Yes?'

His sharp look of eager inquiry almost convinced Kerr that here was a fraud, a trick. It gave him the impression that Doriennet was deliberately talking like a crazy fool to hoodwink him, and was extremely anxious to succeed.

'Certainly I shall try, Mr Doriennet.' He pressed the bell, Doriennet leaned back and waited, frowning, and Kerr was actually watching his eyes when Mold came. 'When Miss Dacre arrives, Mold, let me know.'

'She is here, sir.'

'Oh – ' Kerr looked ruefully towards Doriennet. He had seen not the slightest change in the other's expression, and he was reasonably sure that the name Dacre meant nothing to the man from Vallena. 'Mr Doriennet, what you tell me makes me put off an important appointment. If you will excuse me for a moment – '

Doriennet smiled blandly.

'For the lady. It ees a pleasure, Mistah Kerr!'

'Thank you.' Kerr slipped out of the room, and Mold closed the door. Kerr's expression held all the warmth and love of a man greeting his fiancée, but his words were those of a Department agent.

'Sorry, Lois – but get Craigie from the nearest call-box, and tell him to have a man round here in ten minutes. He's to follow the oddity who comes out of this flat wearing a fur coat. It looks as though you and I might have other work on foot. Tell Craigie the cove comes from AKA.'

Lois Dacre nodded, and turned towards the door. She was the coolest and most capable woman Kerr had ever known, and the most lovable. He flashed her a smile as she sped on her way, and then he returned to M. Jules Doriennet.

He had a queer, almost frightening feeling that something might have happened to the man while he had been out of the room, but apart from helping himself to more lager, Doriennet appeared to be still in complete possession of his faculties and health.

'It ees done, yes? She is understanding, that one?'

'Most,' smiled Kerr, and then Doriennet saw an entirely different man. Instead of listening Kerr talked, and most of his words took the form of questions. At the end of ten minutes Kerr knew most of what there was to know, assuming he had been answered truthfully. It appeared that 'they' had made certain demands from Doriennet a year before, demands which had also been issued to other firms. He had had orders to send poor quality goods to England, or to ship wrong consignments: be it margarine for butter, or deal for oak, or culture pearls for watches.

That information seemed to be in keeping with the craziness of the whole scheme, and Kerr was convinced of its truth. No man would imagine stuff like that. Had Doriennet claimed to have been ordered to ship gunpowder instead of boracic acid there would have been good reason to believe it was a fake interview, but concerning ordinary commerce, it seemed to make conclusive evidence.

'I see. Well, Mr Doriennet, we've kept the most important to last. Who are "they"?'

Doriennet shrugged his shoulders beneath the great bear of a coat.

'So. Mr. Kerr, you will laugh, you will anger, you will say I lie – *but I do not know*. These orders I have had, come always by letter. And as I say no, so I lose things. I am robbed, I have the bad luck, a ship ees sunk, an insurance company will not pay me. One – two – three – *a hundred*! And two days ago, I say: I will find them. I have a letter, it ees delivered by hand. I follow the man. I find the office he visit. I hear him say he will be there again next day. I go again, taking this time the office nex' door, it ees empty. I hear the talk of killing me, and killing you, an' this man Craigie who they also fear, and I come. I fly, by the air. I know they have finished me. My mon-ee it ees gone. My life, I still have it. I am afraid, perhaps, but I wish to stay alive. I come here, because they say your address. Craigie's – they say not his. But of those men I recognise none. I say only this – one, he is so ver' tall, he is taller than me! Six feet one half, I swear! Now – now you understand?'

Kerr thought he did.

Here was a business man who had been sent remarkable orders, had disobeyed them, and had been systematically made to pay for it. Doriennet possessed greater sticking powers than most, but the final talk of killing had been too much for him. It might, of course, be a clever red herring, yet the very bizarreness of it made it seem genuine.

'I think so, Mr Doriennet. I will certainly make inquiries. But how shall I get in touch with you?'

M. Jules Doriennet's face altered surprisingly. From earnestness it developed cunning – the cunning of a man who was not used to subterfuge, but was delighting in his cleverness.

'Ah-ha! I tell no one, Mistah Kerr – not even you. How else can I save myself? It is all prepared, my disappearance! And – '

Doriennet suddenly pulled a large gold watch from his pocket. He jumped up, gathered the voluminous fur coat close about him, and hurried for the door.

Kerr did not try to stop him. Lois would have had the message delivered by now, and Craigie had had good time to work in. Kerr stepped to the window. He saw Doriennet hurrying like a whirlwind along Brook Street, and a well-dressed man leave the wheel of a large car and follow him. Kerr recognised the motorist as a Department Z agent named Trale.

Kerr suddenly moved from the window, went out of the room faster than Doriennet, grabbed a hat and was soon in Brook Street. Neither of the others was out of sight, nor was the third man who had inspired Kerr to move so fast.

The third man was also following M. Jules Doriennet and he was far, far taller than the average. At least six feet and a half, thought Kerr, and therefore possessing at least one physical feature of the only member of the 'they' whom Doriennet had been able to describe.

Chapter 2

A Shock For Freddie

'Tumpty-tum, tumpty-tum, tum-te-*tum*!' carolled Mr. Frederick Kingham, knotting a carefully-chosen tie while holding an unimportant chin well forward, and craning a neck inclined to thinness. 'That's about it I fancy, thank heaven it isn't one of those places where one has to dress. Tumpty-tum, *tump* – come in!'

The door was decorously opened by a middle-aged man dressed in sombre black. Bennet, thought Freddie Kingham, had probably served royalty in his time. Bit of a come down, come to think of it, to wait on a prominent industrialist and that industrialist's not so successful relations. Bennet, though, was a good sort. He could be relied on for a fiver at a pinch. Odd, how all the crowd at Lane House were good sorts. Even Uncle Matt and the pantry boy.

''Lo, Bennet. Come in.'

'There is a young lady to see you, sir.'

'Young what? I don't believe it, Bennet, my conscience is quite clear. It must be my brother she's after, and he's probably halfway up the Mambesi River by now.'

'She distinctly said "Mr. *Frederick* Kingham," sir.'

Freddie straightened his coat collar, and moved to the door.

'Odd. I can't think of any girl wanting to see me. You said young. Any other qualifications?'

'A personable young lady, sir.'

'Hmm.' Freddie twisted his neck again and managed to catch a reflection in the mirror. He was nothing if not honest, and he knew he could do with an inch of Uncle Matt's chin, and a stone or so of his father's bulk. Otherwise the general result was not too bad. 'Where is she, Bennet?'

'In the morning-room, sir.'

'Did she say what she wanted?'

'She said the business was strictly private, sir.'

'Looks worse and worse,' beamed Freddie. 'Well, I'd better get it over. Be at hand in case I need any help, won't you?'

Still humming under his breath, Freddie made his way towards the morning-room of Lane House. Lane House was one of those country places which were more than villas and yet not quite mansions. It was big but not overpowering, and more than comfortably furnished. At six o'clock that evening – the evening of the day when Bob Kerr had talked with Mr Doriennet of Vallena – Freddie, glimpsing the chaste lawns and riotous flower beds outside, told himself again that life was good. And to think that three years before he had come down from Cambridge, to find his father broke to the wide and quarrelling with Uncle Matt, the provider of the Kingham comfort; not to mention his own perilously spartan diet for most of a summer and a winter.

Freddie, who was not equipped for the ordinary trials of working life, had found it more than hard to endure. In time the quarrel between his father and Matthew Horn (his mother's brother) had been patched up, and for nearly two years now Freddie had worked five days a week in the offices of Horn, Beddle, Graham & Co., importers and exporters, and spent the other two days at Lane House.

Full of cheer and well-being, he opened the door of the morning-room and had something of a shock: why, damn it, the girl was almost beautiful! The way she smiled at him for instance, made his heart flutter.

Freddie hurried forward.

'I hope you'll forgive me, Mr Kingham.' He would have forgiven anyone who could smile at him like that. 'I had to come unofficially, and could not give the butler my card.'

Despite his request, she was standing close to him. Her perfume, whatever it was, had a subtlety Freddie was experienced enough to admire. With the sun shining on her hair like that she – Good God!

For Freddie Kingham had glanced from her hair to the card she had given him, and he saw:

Miss L. I. Dale
Special Branch,
Scotland Yard, S.W.1.

'S-Scotland *Yard*!' breathed Freddie Kingham, groping for cigarettes. 'I – smoke? No, I've got a match. But what on earth do you want to see *me* about?'

Miss L. I. Dale, whom Bob Kerr would have identified as Lois Dacre, of Craigie's Department Z, smiled again as she sat down opposite the youthful member of the firm of Horn, Beddle and Graham.

'Well, it's not too easy to explain, Mr Kingham. I must say at once that I have to rely on your discretion, and not a word of this conversation must be repeated. Can you promise that?'

Freddie frowned unhappily.

'We-ll. It rather depends what it's about, you know –'

Lois Dacre changed her opinion of the man in front of her. Nine out of ten, at his age, would have promised to hold their tongues for ever, and afterwards blurted her questions out at the first opportunity. If this man promised secrecy he would maintain it: that was refreshing.

'I quite understand,' she assured him. 'But before we talk, I wonder if you'll make sure we can't be overheard?'

Freddie looked startled.

'Good Lord, that's all right. Walls here are as thick as blazes, and the door's curtained. Absolute privacy guaranteed. But look here – '

'It's going to sound absurd, and you'll wonder why I've talked like I have, but I'm really anxious that your Uncle should know nothing of this for a while, Mr Kingham. No, it's nothing criminal, it's merely something we are investigating for another firm, and the trails happen to cross.'

Freddie licked his lips. Here was a peach of a girl and a spot of police inquiries, both things in which he had always specialised in a purely detached and independent manner.

'Carry on, please.'

'Thanks. You work at the offices of Horn, Beddle and Graham, don't you?'

'Yes. Have done for a couple of years, more or less. I'm a kind of liaison officer or tact merchant between departments and the customers.'

Lois Dacre laughed. Kingham was a refreshing youngster.

'Then you've been overworked lately, haven't you?'

'Overworked?' Freddie wondered if she were pulling his leg. 'Well, hardly. Been a few spots of bother one way and the other, but generally I can't say I'm put on. Folks are pretty decent on the whole, you know.'

'I was thinking of the consignments of goods you've had recently from the exporters of Baj.'

Lois spoke guilelessly, yet watching for reaction; she found what she was looking for. Freddie started, and then frowned. She saw that he possessed a stronger character than she had supposed.

'I see. How on earth you got on to that I don't know, but it's certainly been the bane of my life. Lost us a packet in orders, too. A messy business. Clocks,' broke off Freddie with a grimace, 'when we ordered *tie-presses*, and that's a mild one. Soap for margarine once, and – but still, you seem to know all about it.'

Lois shook her head.

'I don't, but I've heard a little, and I want to learn more. As a matter of fact there's one thing you can perhaps tell me right away, and another you might be able to get for me. First, how many Vallenian firms have supplied the right things lately?'

Freddie scratched his chin.

'We-ll, in point of fact, only Doriennet's have been consistently on the mark, and we had a cable in today saying they're going out of business. Looks as though we'll have to close down with our orders over there. What's the other thing?'

Lois Dacre hesitated before she spoke.

'Mr Kingham, this inquiry is an unusual one, and we are anxious that no principals of the firms concerned should know of it. I'm trying to get a complete list of the wrongly-shipped goods, and all the firms concerned. Would that be possible, do you think?'

Freddie looked a little put out.

'Without Uncle Matt knowing, eh? Well, it could be done, but I'm afraid I can't do it. You must see that. He is my uncle, you know, and a pretty good sort.'

Lois nodded sympathetically.

'Of course. I hardly expected you to say yes, and later on we shall probably have to get the particulars from other firms as well as yourselves. Don't worry about it. Now one other question, and I needn't trouble you again. Have you ever come in contact with a Vallenian – or anyone Vallenian – who is abnormally tall? I'm afraid that's the only description I have of him at the moment.'

'You mean Kryn,' said Freddie with certainty.

'Kryn?'

'K-R-Y-N. He's a kind of floating commission man, if you know what I mean. Doesn't work for any particular firm, but often slides in with a bit of commission. For instance, we might want a dozen gross of clocks, and if we get half a gross extra – at his request – we can buy 'em for a much lower price than he could get a single half-gross lot. Following me?'

'Yes, quite well.'

'Good. Kryn gets us to order that extra half-gross, and we sell to him at the price we pay. No profit in it for us, but a bit later we might want a small quantity of a certain article, and he can get them from another exporter or importer at a low price – much less than we'd have to pay. It's a bit complicated,' said Freddie considerately, 'but you get used to it.'

'I think I've got it,' said Lois, demurely.

Freddie did not know the jubilation that was filling Agent Eleven of Department Z. Lois Dacre had hardly expected to get information so promptly about the tall man whom the remarkable M. Jules Doriennet, of Baj, had mentioned. Moreover she had obtained confirmation in many ways of the Vallenian's story, sufficiently corroborative at least to make it more likely to be true than false.

Freddie Kingham beamed. He had forgotten that it was half-past six, and that at six-forty-five he was due at the house of friends, fifteen miles away. He could not have said it in so many words, but he was experiencing a complete sense of contentment. He was reminded of the earlier days of his youth, when he had once met and spoken to the celebrated and god-like cricketer of the year.

'Good work, Miss Dale! Not everyone gets into it as quickly as you do – it took me a month,' he added with disarming frankness. 'But I was never really bright. Look here, what put you on to me?'

Lois said that the caretaker of the offices had known Mr Frederick Kingham worked there and also lived with his uncle, the firm's only remaining original partner. But she failed to say a lot that would have greatly interested Freddie.

* * *

In the three and a half hours since Doriennet had left 77g Brook Street, many things had happened with the speed and thoroughness that characterised the agents of Department Z at work. The agent named Trale had followed Doriennet as far as Heston, where the Vallenian had taken a private plane, and started for the Lord knew where. Trale had taken the number, make and description of the plane, discovered the name of the pilot from the offices, learned that Doriennet, who had booked the bus in his right name, was officially going to Scotland, and telephoned all this to Gordon Craigie, who had sat in his Whitehall office waiting for the developments to take on some pattern.

Bob Kerr, meanwhile, had passed an interesting hour.

The extremely tall man, whose name it later turned out was Kryn, followed Doriennet as far as the turning towards Heston Airport. Both he and Doriennet had used taxis: Kerr had commandeered the powerful car that Trale had left behind, and Trale had managed to get a small Frazer Nash.

Apparently Kryn had been satisfied that Doriennet needed no further following.

He had taken the same taxi back to Piccadilly, alighted at the Circus, and then walked to the Riltaz Hotel. Kerr had taken the car by easy stages to the hotel, waited five minutes and then discovered – because he was known to the receptionist – that the tall man had booked a room in the name of Jacobs, and that he had never been to the hotel before.

This Kerr telephones at once to Craigie who detailed two men – a certain, long, weary-looking and well-dressed gentleman known as Wallace Davidson, and another almost as tall, named Robert Carruthers – to visit the Riltaz Hotel and watch 'Jacobs' or his visitors. He had also been in touch with Lois Dacre, who had visited Scotland Yard to discover what she could of Doriennet's business associates in England.

The Yard had had little trouble in discovering that Messrs. Horn, Beddle and Graham of Tooley Street, S.E., had for some time been Doriennet's best English customer.

Armed with Kerr's knowledge of the tall man (through Craigie) Lois had visited Lane House, situated some mile and a half from Camberley High Street, and an hour-and-a-half's run from London.

Here she learned what little Freddie knew of Kryn, and then, to Freddie's sorrow, took her leave. She had hinted at the likelihood of needing his help again, had left her private phone number and her Audley Street address, and suggested that if anyone wondered why she had called, he should tell them that she was an old acquaintance of his.

Regretfully, Freddie watched her driving off in a small

Morris. Halfway up the stairs he ran into Bennet.

Delighted with his diplomatic role he called out:

'I did know her, Bennet – very old friend of my palmier days – quite O.K. if she should call here again.'

'Very good, sir.'

Freddie went to his room, refilled his cigarette case, telephoned his friends at Farnham that he would be late, and went blithely out to the garage.

It was some way from the house, and he was whistling happily as he unlocked the doors. He hooked them back, and was about to slip into the driving seat of his Singer Sports model, when he caught sight of the thing.

Freddie stopped, and went very still.

At first glance it was a coat. An unfamiliar coat, of a lightish brown fur, bundled into a corner and difficult to see. But as he stared he saw feet poking from one end, and a head from the other – a head that it was difficult to recognise, for the top seemed to have been blown right off.

Chapter 3

Things Move

Freddie Kingham's first reaction was to be sick.

His face had lost all colour, and he found it impossible to move. This odd, paralytic effect on his limbs scared him. He remembered feeling something like it when an army tank had crashed into his last car, and he had seen it coming without being able to do the first thing in self-defence. Then, as now, he had escaped with little more than shock.

But – but good God! It was ghastly!

He moved his right hand tremblingly. Somehow he disliked leaving the thing there, but he had to go. He turned his eyes away, and then caught sight of a maid outside the kitchen door.

His first call was a croak, and then his voice grew firmer. The maid heard him, and drew near; a young, chubby-faced little baggage always ready for an amorous approach.

'Yes, Mr Frederick?'

She must have seen the pallor of his cheeks, for her hopeful smile disappeared.

'Are – are you all right, sir? Shall I – '

'Cut in, and tell Bennet to bring Mr Horn, *at once*,' said Freddie, more steadily than he had expected. 'Don't lose a second.'

The girl was startled into acting promptly. Freddie saw her disappear, pushed his hand through his mouse-coloured hair, and lit a cigarette.

It tasted like blotting paper. Damn it, why didn't the others come?

Then he saw Bennet and Matthew Horn striding from the house. Bennet showed no expression. Matthew Horn looked prepared to be annoyed or angered.

That, however, was his perpetual expression.

He was no taller than his nephew, but very thick-set. People seeing him for the first time were amused, until they looked into a dark, rather forbidding face with a wide, close-cropped moustache. The moustache gave his face a more ferocious expression than really suited it, and his surprisingly clear and pleasant blue eyes came as something of a shock.

His voice, when it came, was cultured, well-modulated and authoritative.

'Well now, Freddie, what's the trouble?'

Kingham lowered his cigarette with a hand that trembled.

'Sorry – Uncle. It's pretty – beastly. In the garage.'

'My dear boy – '

'A dead man,' Kingham said faintly.

Bennet's mouth gaped, and he started back as though he was about to be assaulted. Horn's only change was a narrowing of his eyes.

'All right, old boy. Where is it?'

'In the corner of the – garage,' Freddie muttered. 'I really can't – can't face it again. Shall I – phone the police?'

'Stay just where you are,' said Matthew Horn.

He walked forward, surprisingly sprightly for a man of his bulk and age. Bennet lagged behind him. Freddie saw them disappear into the garage, one after the other. They did not disappear for long, and when they came out Bennet's pallow had increased, while Matthew Horn's face was grim.

'Stay here, Freddie – no need to go nearer the garage – and make sure no one approaches. I'll send for Browning, and then telephone the police.'

He started off at a jog trot, Bennet following him, to the house. In a couple of minutes a tall, ungainly looking man dressed in a loose tweed suit considerably the worse for wear, arrived. This was Browning, the Lane House odd-job man.

Browning had been the gardener's boy until the outbreak of the war. Six months of Flanders had given him six years in hospital with shell-shock. Matthew Horn had afterwards taken him back in his employ. Although Browning's nerve had been shattered for some things – he could not drive a car, for instance, and he hated any kind of gardening calling for knives or shears – when there had been a fatal accident near the house he had shown no more than the normal reaction to the sight of death and mutililation.

'Bit o' trouble, sir?'

'Looks like it,' Freddie agreed. 'Don't go in. You haven't seen any strangers about, have you?'

Browning scratched his chin.

'Well, yes an' no, sir. They comes orf that footpath by the fence rather a lot, sir – arter the apples. No saying *who* might have come in or gorn out, come to think.'

Freddie remembered that there was a small gateway leading from the side of the garage to a public footpath. The gate was easily opened, and the gardeners had a running feud with the local lads bent on rifling the orchard. Certainly anyone could have entered the garage.

But how had the man in the fur coat got there?

His nerve steadier, Freddie began to think out whys and wherefores. And then suddenly he remembered the woman from Scotland Yard. *She* was a complete stranger, and she had been at hand.

No! He was going crackers, a woman of that type would not have done a thing like murder. Anyhow, she was working for the police. By Jove, inquiring about Doriennet, too! This looked hot! When the local police arrived he could –

Freddie suddenly remembered that he had promised not to talk of her visit. He was a man of his word, and he did not persuade himself that it would be justifiable to break it now. Pity she would not be home yet, but he could leave a message. She had been gone half-an-hour now, and ought to be in London before eight o'clock.

* * *

At a quarter to eight, Bob Kerr was sitting in a roomy office just off Whitehall.

It was barely furnished, particularly at the far end, where a few filing cabinets – increasing year by year – a table with several telephones, and a dictaphone were standing. At the other end, clustered round a slow-burning coal fire, were two easy chairs, several hard-back ones, a cupboard with the door closed but containing a remarkable collection of oddments from foodstuffs to clean collars, and two small tables.

It was the office of Department Z.

Gordon Craigie, sitting back now in the easiest of the easy chairs, spent so much time there that he needed a section to serve as living quarters. Craigie's coffee – he drank it throughout the day – was famous, but Craigie himself was known as the Chief of Department Z only to a few. In recent years the few had increased. He had conducted various campaigns, in international and national affairs, that had brought him unwelcome publicity: to foreign powers even a certain notoriety.

In England, however, he was little known.

The Cabinet knew him, and some of its members cursed him for the frankness of his comments on their actions. Craigie sometimes said that for every mistake they made he had a week of sleepless nights. But he was essentially non-political, and the more honest members of changing cabinets appreciated his frankness, and liked him.

So did the agents of Department Z.

His lean and narrow face was turned now in the direction of Kerr, who had just come in.

'Sorry I had to mess up your afternoon, Bob. I phoned the Burkes and said you couldn't get to them. A queer show.'

Kerr thumbed his jaw.

'Queer's the word for it. I'm damned if I'm sure yet whether the man was a lunatic or not, but what Lois has telephoned from Camberley suggests he wasn't. So some gentlemen in Vallena – including this Mr Kryn, alias

Jacobs – would like to see us dead, eh?'

Craigie smiled.

'Well, they're not the first people to do so. I'm a lot concerned with *why* they do it.'

'Any ideas?' asked Kerr.

'Plenty. Haven't you?'

Kerr scowled.

'Well, the usual round, of course. But AKA – what the blazes does AKA want to mess about with us for? A tinpot little state which doesn't know its own mind. An unpopular puppet Prince, a play-girl Princess – '

'That's the whole thing,' said Craigie, taking a meerschaum from a rack near the fireplace. 'Someone inside the State does know his – or her – own mind. That someone wants to upset trade relations with England, and as far as I can see have precious nearly succeeded in doing it. They've chosen a novel way,' added Craigie with a chuckle. 'I can imagine the thoughts of a man who order braces and gets powder-puffs! All the same, it's the other angle that makes it more serious, Bob.'

Kerr nodded.

'The reports you've had from Vallena. What's the gist of them?'

Craigie stuffed his meerschaum with slow deliberation.

'Well – when I telephoned you earlier, they were just interesting. There's talk of a faction over in Vallena that want to join the Hitler *regime*. There aren't many countries without a party with that bee in their bonnets, but Vallena's been pretty free from it up to now. The only thing Vallenians seemed really interested in is their Princess.'

Kerr sniffed, thinking of the activities of the Princess Katrina of Vallena, which had done more than anything else to make her country's name familiar. Estranged from an unpopular husband, she led a hectic life in the casinos of the world; Kerr knew she flew her own plane; so did every man and woman able to read.

'Bit far removed from Germany, isn't it?'

'Well, on the surface perhaps. Tucked there at the foot of the Carpathians, it's got Poland on the north, Czechoslovakia on the west, and Rumania south and east. The Black Sea is the nearest big water-way, but from what we've seen, most of their stuff is shipped across country to Holland or Belgium, and put on steamer there. Not much of an obvious contact with Germany, I agree. The obvious indirect one is Poland.'

Kerr frowned.

'It looks too early to size it up yet, Gordon. Is this Nazi talk the only suspicious kind you've heard?'

'There's a strong faction for linking up with the U.S.S.R.,' Craigie told him, 'and that looks like the real trouble. A repeat of the Spain business, differing only geographically. White versus Red – Democracy versus Dictatorship – mostly,' added Craigie with a rare touch of bitterness. 'One man's greed versus another's.'

Kerr's eyes shone for a moment: Craigie rarely let himself go.

'Was that why you thought of sending me out there?'

Craigie poked the mouthpiece of his meerschaum towards his chief agent.

'Partly, Bob. But chiefly because *both* parties in Vallena have been dealing with the Associated International Industry Corporation, a beautifully high-sounding name that covers – '

'Our Adam Criff, eh? That's the angle.'

Craigie nodded. Kerr thought fleetingly of a Mr Adam Criff, who had at one time figured in the Italo-Abyssinian conflict, later in the Franco revolution, still later and more profitably in the Chino-Japanese war. Mr Adam Criff's interests seemed to follow strife, and obviously Craigie was worried lest Mr Criff encouraged strife in Vallena.

The odd thing about Criff was that he did not appear to be connected with armaments. Even in his earliest appearance in the Paraguay-Bolivia horror he had concentrated on foodstuffs. An odder thing was that he was young-middle-aged, and increasingly popular with upper crust society.

Kerr was thinking fast.

So Craigie had had reports from agents in Baj and other places suggesting that there was a possibility of a flare-up between the two sides in Vallena, and Adam Criff was interested. That would be ample justification for sending his chief agent over.

'It's connected all right,' he said, 'and this fiddling business with English-bought merchandise has a place. I – hallo, visitors.'

Nothing was heard, but in the mantelpiece a small green light showed. Craigie took extreme – and some people thought absurd – precautions to make sure he was not approached unknowingly. Ostensibly there was no door to Department Z. Actually there were five or six, opening from different passages in the maze of Government buildings of which the office was a part, and all operated on a sliding panel principle. Perhaps it amused Craigie.

'From the street,' Craigie said.

No one could press the concealed bell outside without knowing where it was, and only Craigie's agents and one or two Yard men knew that. Craigie leaned forward to the fireplace, pressed a button that seemed to be part of an ornate cream tile, and both he and Kerr looked round.

Kerr jumped up quickly, as Lois Dacre entered. The door slid to as she reached him, but it was Craigie who spoke first.

'What is it?'

'Doriennet,' said Lois simply. 'I've just telephoned young Kingham. He called me an hour or so after I left Horn's place. Doriennet's down there, murdered it seems, and certainly dead. Who's coming to investigate with me?'

* * *

Just fifteen minutes later, Mr Wallace Davidson and Mr Robert Carruthers, relieved from their watch at the Riltaz Hotel by other agents, bundled into Carruthers' Lagonda.

Carruthers was driving, and at Hyde Park Corner he saw a Frazer Nash, holding Kerr and Lois Dacre.

Davidson smiled, somewhat wearily.

'Caught 'em, old son. Going to try and get there first?'

'Try?' snorted Carruthers. 'That wreck of Bob's can't do more than seventy, it ought to be taken out of service. I wonder what's happening?'

'Plenty, or we wouldn't have to move so fast. Cancel all social arrangements, Carry. Damn it, I wish we'd had time for a quick one, I'm thirsty.'

'If we get well ahead we could stop at a local,' said Carruthers hopefully.

Davidson looked cheered.

'It's an idea, but you can't drink while you're driving, Carry, it's not done. Illegal or something, isn't it? Know the pub?'

'The White Star, Camberley.'

'Good man,' said Davidson heartily.

In the next traffic block he scribbled the name of the pub on a sheet from his notebook, and Carruthers – working in perfect accord – managed to draw level with Kerr's Frazer Nash at a Hammersmith Broadway stoppage. Davidson flicked the note over. It struck Lois Dacre on the cheek, but she gave no sign that she had received it, until some five minutes later she retrieved it from the floor.

'Any developments?' Kerr asked her.

'Probably, I – the *louts*! They're stopping at a pub in Camberley. Bob, how on earth they manage to keep going with Craigie I don't know, they must be drunk half their time.'

Kerr laughed.

'Don't worry about them, Lois, they always come up to scratch. If they're not thirsty they always pretend to be. It's a kind of affectation. We'll hoot three times as we go past.' He glanced at Lois Dacre's somewhat indignant face – she had worked once before for the Department, but had not yet managed to understand the peculiar nature of Craigie's band of hearty young agents. They had a habit of acting the fool, more particularlarly when there was danger in the offing.

Not knowing the wrath they had called down on their heads, Carruthers and Davidson made the run to the White Star, Camberley, eight minutes faster than Kerr. Time, in fact, for two quick ones. They were actually outside the pub before the Frazer Nash appeared, and true to policy Davidson merely winked an eye in recognition.

Moving with an apparent lethargy that was deceptive, Davidson reached the Lagonda before Carruthers. A small, red-faced man in a suit the wrong shade of blue reached an innocent-looking Morris 10 before them. The man in the blue suit appeared to have no connection with Department Z, but he took the same turnings towards Lane House.

Suddenly, devastatingly, he ceased to be an insignificant little man sedately driving a family car. In a superb demonstration of ace driving, he squeezed past the Frazer Nash, forcing Kerr's bus well over. As he went past he swung round in his seat.

Carruthers saw the start of the mad drive, and promptly switched on his headlights. In the glare they could see the little man, with an automatic in his left hand, and his right hand on the wheel.

Davidson swore, and his hand flew to his pocket as flame came from the little man's gun. For a moment there was uproar, and as Carruthers jammed on his brakes he had a horrible feeling that he heard Lois Dacre scream.

Chapter 4

Mr Criff and Others

In the glare of the Lagonda's headlights the whole scene was bizarrely clear: the little man shooting, Kerr wrenching at his wheel, Lois Dacre falling below the level of the windscreen. Then the man in the blue suit became suddenly aware that the second car-load of men were working with Kerr.

It seemed to terrify him.

He loosed his remaining bullets wildly, and dropped down to the steering, but he might as well have pulled up at once. Davidson aimed at the rear wheels of the Morris. In that breathless rush past the Frazer Nash even a driver of such superb skill had been forced to slow down, for he had been shooting as well.

One rear tyre and another burst with a roar that seemed like dynamite. The Morris lurched to the far side of the road, while the Frazer Nash shuddered to a standstill, its front wheels locked in the hedge. There was no room for Carruthers to get the Lagonda through.

It was not necessary.

The little man in the wrong shade of blue seemed to realise that though there was no hope of driving away, there was a very small chance of escaping on foot. Before his car had stopped, he leapt for the hedge, and Carruthers saw him scrambling over.

'Get the little runt,' he snapped.

Davidson fired twice in quick succession.

Carruthers was already hurrying towards the car. He wanted to make sure that Lois Dacre was not badly hurt, and he left the gunman to Davidson.

Still with the headlights illuminating the scene, he saw Lois slowly straighten up.

Carruthers beamed.

'Foxing, eh? I'm disgusted with you, Miss Dacre, I'd already worked out a startling paragraph for the evening papers, in the hopes of collecting a bit for the exclusive story, of course. You all right?'

Lois looked at him scathingly.

'What a crazy fool you are. Yes – I don't think my hat's any more use, though.'

It was not. Two bullets had decorated it with small round holes. Carruther's good spirits were damped a little, while Kerr's expression was thunderous.

'Blasted little rat. Good thing you were behind, Carry.'

'Good thing Wally was thirsty, or we'd have been in front,' Carruthers said. 'Red Face didn't think we were in it, and expected us just to find the bodies. Quick work, eh?'

'I'm lucky,' said Kerr soberly, 'but Doriennet, poor devil – ah, well.'

They were all out of the cars now. The Frazer Nash's front wheels were too buckled for the car to be of any immediate use, and the Morris looked considerably the worse for wear. But the point of main interest was Wally Davidson.

He had extricated the wounded gunman from the hedge, where he had fallen when Davidson had shot him in the leg.

Carruthers called out: 'Let's look him over.'

Kerr broke in, almost sharply: 'There's time later for that, Carry. Run through his pockets, Bob, and see what he's carrying. Wally, we've got to lift the Morris over this side of the road, and get past. We're wanted up the lane.'

'Navvying now,' groaned Davidson.

The Morris was not as heavy as it might have been, and by taking the front first, and then the back, they soon had it on one side.

Kerr waited just long enough to lift the bonnet.

'Think it might go off?' asked Davidson.

'Super-charged,' said Kerr briefly. 'Let's get going.'

A thoughtful quartette and a badly frightened gunman who had forgotten the pain in his legs and was wondering what these hard-faced but oddly flippant men were going to do with him, were loaded into the Lagonda, and Carruthers squeezed through the gap.

'Anyone know how much further?'

'Half a mile or a little more,' Lois said. 'the road gets narrower, and there are some nasty turns.'

'What fun,' said Carruthers. 'I can't wait.' But presently he too lapsed into silence. There was more than enough to be thoughtful about.

Kerr thought more quickly than any of the others, and he saw three things significant enough for concern. The first, and least important, was the fact that beneath the guise of an ordinary Morris 10, the little man had been driving a super-charged car, capable of travelling at a hundred miles an hour or more. Small wonder the man had managed to pass the Frazer Nash!

The second was that Red Face must have been waiting for their arrival at Camberley, and recognised them when they passed the White Star. Not so good. But he had not recognised either Davidson or Carruthers, both well-known members of the Department. This suggested that only Kerr had been identified.

The third point was that Red Face had been entrusted to carry out this job alone, and that suggested that the active fighting forces of the men who worked – presumably – for Kryn was not a strong one. Otherwise there would have been two men on this job.

But the cool nerve of it!

Red Face, of course, had reckoned on having only the one car to handle. He had followed Kerr, and working on the assumption that Kerr would have put such behaviour down to road-hogging, raced past him and then opened fire. But for the arrival and interference of the Lagonda, it would have gone very badly for Kerr and Lois Dacre.

Kerr was conscious of an acute feeling of dissatisfaction with himself. Thanks to Doriennet he had been warned in good time, and he should have been prepared for trouble. But even when he had seen that the Morris was taking the same road as himself, he had thought of nothing more than the possibility of being followed. An open attack had simply not occurred to him.

He looked affectionately at Lois.

It would take more than a single attack and a passing danger, no matter how acute, seriously to worry her, he knew. He remembered the time, six months back, when she had been shot nearly to death. Even after that she had not hesitated to continue working for Craigie. He was proud of her, but that she should be exposed to such desperate hazards worried him.

Kerr jerked himself out of reminiscence. Doriennet had been murdered, as far as he could judge, and there were other things to be cleared up. Adam Criff's part in this game. Kryn's – whoever he was. And the reason for Doriennet's presence at the house of Mr Matthew Horn.

* * *

Kerr made his report to Craigie five hours later. Lois had gone home, and the other two were resting, but every available agent on Craigie's list had been warned to prepare for action.

The local police had been told of Kerr's coming, and had accepted without question his control of the situation. Freddie Kingham, Matthew Horn, and all members of the household, including Joshua Kingham, had been interrogated. Freddie's father, an artist of sorts, had proved to be a vast man with an echoing voice and the barest modicum of common sense.

As far as Kerr had been able to judge, none of them had expected Doriennet at the house. Horn's account had appeared straightforward, and the servants' statements, Kerr said, seemed honest enough, The only one who might be worth watching was the butler, Bennet, who fitted into his role almost too perfectly.

'In short,' said Kerr, 'there seems a reasonable chance that the poor devil of a Vallenian was going to Horn for help, and was murdered on the way. But there's another implication, Gordon. Kryn – we'll say he's our man for the sake of a name – might have wanted Doriennet to be found at Lane House, to make things awkward for Matthew Horn.'

Craigie pursed his lips.

'A possibility, certainly. At all events, the aeroplane that took Doriennet from Heston landed at Farnham according to the pilot, at Doriennet's urgent request.'

'Did Doriennet seem worried?'

'Fidgety as hell, according to the pilot,' said Craigie. 'After they'd landed at Farnham, Doriennet took a taxi from the station, as far as the end of Lane House drive. The taximan says he was told exactly where to stop.'

Kerr whistled.

'That looks very much as if Doriennet had been in England before.'

'I certainly don't think he told us all the truth.'

'Seems to implicate Horn, too.' Kerr said. 'Who's watching him?'

'Dodo Trale.'

Silence dropped on them for some minutes.

There were far too many complications for Kerr's liking. He remembered Doriennet's words. According to the man, the people who had been with Kryn when he had eavesdropped, Kerr was the one who worried them most. That suggested that Kryn was scared of the resources of Department Z, and had planned to get rid of the agent he believed to be the most dangerous.

Kerr's lips parted in a reflective smile.

Kryn evidently had no idea of the real power of the Department. Men came and went, but like the brook in Tennyson's poem, the Department went on, effective, ruthless, remorseless as ever. He might die tomorrow, but it would not seriously affect the working of Craigie's branch of the Secret Service.

But Kerr saw no reason for dying unnecessarily.

He scowled when he remembered Doriennet's love of life, and the pitiful figure of the man bundled into a corner of the garage at Lane House.

The poor blighter had been so confident of his arrangements, too. Kerr said tersely:

'Gordon, Doriennet had made plans, and he went directly to Horn's place. What does that suggest to you?'

'That Horn was going to help him.'

'Yes – but Horn denies it. Says he hadn't expected to see the man, and had never seen him before.'

'We'll try and find out when Doriennet was last in England,' Craigie said, tapping out his pipe. 'I wouldn't trust Horn too far. But the little fellow you managed to catch could be significant.'

'Red Face.' Kerr screwed up his nose. 'We-ell – I'd put him down simply as a hired killer. Whoever sent him guessed I'd be in the Lane House direction soon after Doriennet's death was discovered.'

Craigie nodded.

'That suggests that they knew he'd been to see you.'

'They knew that all right – or Mr Kryn did,' said Kerr. 'Unless I'm a long way out in my reckoning, Kryn knew I followed him, and knows he's being watched now. Are you thinking of hauling him in and trying to make him talk?'

'Not yet,' Craigie said. 'He might lead us to something useful. He's better where he is, as Mr. Jacobs at the Riltaz. A pity Fencer won't – or can't – talk.'

Kerr's face looked bleak.

He had spent half-an-hour at Lane House, with the little red-faced man in the blue suit, who had admitted to the name of Fencer. He was, he said a hired gunman. He had spent some time in America, been shot out, and wandered through the Continent before being hired to go to England. The letter hiring him had not been signed but the postmark had been Paris.

Thereafter, Fencer said, he took orders by letter or telephone. He had rooms in a small Bayswater Hotel, was paid a retaining fee and so much for any special job he did. He had no idea who had talked to him, and could not describe the voice of the man who always gave instructions although now and again a woman spoke, and Fencer described her voice as a razz; apparently he meant attractive. He had been ordered to burn all letters after receiving them, he had obeyed and swore he had committed no other shooting offences in England.

'I'm prepared to swear he doesn't know anything more,' said Kerr.' Nothing he's done will help us – excepting that Kryn now lacks one gunman.'

Craigie nodded.

'It's disappointing, but we can't expect too much. I don't think you'd better go to Vallena yet – it looks as if there's work to be done over here. But you might find out what you can about Adam Criff. I can tell you that he has booked an Airways seat for Poland, leaving tomorrow.'

'It's an odd fact,' said Bob Kerr with a grin, 'but I was thinking about Adam myself. Lois doesn't seem to be known in this show yet. Now if Criff wanted a secretary – '

Craigie smiled and yawned.

'An old, old trick, though it might work. But be careful, Bob. There'll be another packet of reports in the morning, and if you phone through I'll be able to pass the gist of them on. Goodnight.'

Kerr nodded briefly, pressed the button and let himself out. He went to his flat by the shortest route, and he was as sure as he could be that no one had followed him. That probably meant that, or that Kryn had no other attacking forces available at the moment.

Kryn – and Adam Criff.

Oddly similar names, thought Bob Kerr, and then he told himself he was getting too imaginative, took a weak whisky and soda, and turned in, an automatic close to his right hand. The time for taking chances had gone.

* * *

Mr. Adam Criff had not slept at all on Sunday night.

Nor had the two other gentlemen, obviously of non-English extraction, who were with him that evening in his Park Lane flat.

Gregaroff Shirin, as his name suggested, was a Russian. A White Russian, he allowed it to be said with some pride. For many years he had been very poor indeed, but the last twelve months – since Doriennet had started getting instructions and refusing to obey them – he had prospered. He was tall and clean-shaven, his hair close-cropped. Even dressed in an English-cut lounge suit, he gave the impresson of being a professional soldier. Gregaroff Shirin, in fact, could recall the days when he had been a Captain in the Imperial Guard, and a friend of the Tsar.

Karl von Hauf was an entirely different type of man. Fat, short, over-paunched, no one knew where the "von" had come from. He talked very little, and when he did he lisped.

He had been warned a few days before the first of the Berlin purges, and he had very sensibly taken that warning; an Aryan mother not quite cancelling out a Jewish father in the opinion of the Nazi regime.

Gregaroff Shirin, then, a Russian who hated the ruling powers in his native country, and Karl von Hauf, a German who detested the ruling spirits in his own distant land, were consulting with that remarkably polished, handsome and persuasive gentleman known as Adam Criff. Criff loved all countries – he said – and hated none. Towards the end of that long, all-night sitting when policy in a dozen ways had been discussed, he was perilously close to hating representatives of Russia and Germany. The discussion was one involving risk, and Criff might have shown his irritation, for Shirin favoured wild chances and von Hauf excessive caution that was equivalent to stagnancy but for the announcement from a tired valet-butler that her ladyship had called.

Criff started to his feet in surprise.

'Lady *Mondell*?'

'Yes, sir, she – '

Criff's man went no further, for Lady Mondell entered the room behind him without fuss or abruptness. She was a startlingly beautiful woman, as the expression of the three men testified.

'My dear Rene – '

Lady Mondell waved her hand.

'You're a fine fool, Adam.'

'A – fool!' von Hauf gasped. Here was sacrilege of the type that would have meant a concentration camp in the Fatherland. Criff also looked taken aback; only Shirin saw an expression in milady's eyes that told of alarm.

She stripped her gloves off slowly.

'A fool, I said. Otherwise – there wouldn't be one of Craigie's men at the back and one at the front. Understand that, Adam. *Craigie's men.* They're watching you, they've found Doriennet, they've caught Fencer.' She hesitated, her pose of coolness dropping. She took three short, sharp steps towards the trio, her hands outstretched and her eyes pools of fear. 'What are we going to do – what are we going to do? *They've caught us*!'

Chapter 5

Milady Lies

The three men in the room of the Park Lane flat had been successful in entirely different mediums. Adam Criff was essentially an organiser: he might have been called the chief director of the trio, and its campaign, Gregaroff Shirin was the liaison officer, and Karl von Hauf manipulated the one thing for which he had a genius – money. None of these three mediums really called for courage.

Now, at Lady Mondell's words, spoken with fear and appeal, Shirin's fresh-coloured face went fresher, and his hands clenched at his sides, while von Hauf uttered a sound – half-squeak, half-groan – of horror. For both of them knew something of the power of Department Z, and the strength of which its agents were capable.

Criff knew as much if not more, and after the moment of strained silence following the woman's words, his laugh came like a douche of cold water.

'A very melodramatic entry, my dear Rene. I thought you had some bad news.'

'Bad news? Why, my poor – '

'Fool, you've said it twice,' murmured Criff, 'why boggle at a third time?' He stepped to the sideboard, elegant, nonchalant and superbly self-controlled, and poured out a finger of whisky. The gurgle as it fell into the glass echoed clearly. He half-filled it with water, and carried it to Lady Mondell. She took it doubtfully.

'Drink it. You need it.'

Rene Mondell drank it, pushing her head back and screwing her eyes up as it went down. It was odd that she had always made a habit of doing what Criff ordered. People did.

Von Hauf spoke jerkily, his voice higher than usual.

'But Criff – Criff! Vat vill happen, I must say Lady Mondell seems vise, yeth, I – '

'Be quiet,' snapped Criff, and there was a difference in his expression and his voice which sent von Hauf back into his chair abruptly. 'Do you want us to panic in a bad moment? Shirin, pull yourself together.'

The outburst did Criff good.

He had been startled and he was still perturbed by the news that Rene had brought him. It was disquieting, to say the least. He had no idea that the Department agents had got on to him. But he could confer as much as he liked with whom he liked: there was nothing the Department could do against him – yet.

Rene, of course, was always inclined to be hysterical. She kept up so far, and then gave way. One day he would have to teach her a lesson.

Shirin's voice, was hoarse.

'Talk – talk. What are you going to do? Here are agents – men after us – perhaps come for us – '

'And then you'll go for trial and perhaps to prison,' sneered Criff. 'It would be an excellent way of looking after you. Von Hauf, stop squealing!'

There was no doubt then that in their different ways the other three were afraid of him. Rene was sitting back with her eyes half-closed, her expression as she looked towards Criff far from friendly. The whisky, apparently, had cleared her mind, as well as steadying her nerves. She had suddenly seen something that was half-animal in this pleasant-voiced, smiling, indubitably handsome man with – it was reputed – an inconceivable fortune to make him still more eligible.

Von Hauf simply sat back and shivered. Shirin stopped pacing the room, for despite his half-hearted defiance, his fear was obvious.

'Well – since you are so brave, so clever – '

Adam Criff stared at him, and then he laughed lightly. The mask was back, and he looked, again, the man who was such a success in Mayfair drawing-rooms. His dark, short-clipped moustache, his handsome head with the crisp, almost black hair, the well-cut features with the rather sensitive-looking nostrils and the too-shapely lips, seemed to form again. The ugly glint left his brown eyes.

'What idiots we are! You were right, Rene, I am a fool to get alarmed and sharp-tongued over a little thing like this. There is, in fact, nothing at all to worry about. Apologies, my dear! Shirin, help yourself – and von Hauf – to whisky.'

Peace seemed to fall over the quartette, a peace ruffled only by the knowledge in all their minds that the Department men were outside.

Lady Mondell broke the silence.

In repose she looked even lovelier than she had when she had entered. She had dropped her fur coat over the arm of her chair, and her legs, long, slim, sheathed in gossamer, seemed to fascinate Shirin.

'So now we're all friends again, Adam, what are you going to do?'

'Well – it is not so hard. Fencer, you say, is caught. But he knows nothing, and can do no harm. Doriennet has been found. Why not? They had to find him somewhere – was he with Horn, by any chance?'

'No. Fencer shot him near the garage – ' She broke off with a shudder, and Criff brushed the sordid matter of a murder to one side. Rene had never accustomed herself to the fact that murder, particularly when the stakes were high, was sometimes inevitable.

'But on Horn's premises, eh? Excellent work, excellent! Nothing at all points to us, so, apart from the fact that I am suspected of – shall we say? – interest in Vallena, what is there to worry about? You see how stupid it is to panic, my dear? I wonder – yes, I wonder how long they've been there?'

Lady Mondell tapped out the ash of her cigarette thoughtfully.

'Since about three o'clock, as far as the night porter can tell me. I – I recognised them immediately, and I went round to the courtyard to see if there was anyone there. There was – a big man named Loftus. None of Craigie's special agents are there, though.'

'I thought so,' said Criff, complacently. 'Merely a matter of idle curiosity, and as Shirin and von Hauf came here with the utmost caution at ten o'clock last night, no one is likely to know they are here now. You both came the back way?'

He glanced towards Shirin and von Hauf, and they nodded with the alacrity of jack-in-the-boxes. Criff's smile grew even more complacent.

'You see, Rene? No cause for alarm after all.'

Rene Mondell was beginning to think so herself.

In many ways she was a remarkable woman. Not yet thirty, she had passed from the chorus to the position of leading lady on the provincial stage, and from there to espionage work; first in England and then abroad. Her backers, one of whom was Criff, had not found it difficult to make her a stage star. There were some thousands of people, among whom were certain dramatic critics, who believed her to be a good actress. Even those who did not, conceded that with her superb figure, a reasonably good voice and an excellent sense of mimicry she did well enough.

As a leading light of the West End stage, however, she had not shone for long.

Still in the pay of Adam Criff, on a strictly business footing, for despite contrary rumours she was not a lady of loose morals, she had gone to Berlin officially on a holiday – actually to work for Criff. Her object was to get information from a colleague of the Fuhrer's, and she had failed. Criff had hardly expected anything else.

Nor had he expected her to meet Sir Douglas Mondell in Berlin.

Mondell, on the young side of middle age, was the most accomplished liar, lady-killer and dilettante related to the British peerage. He had never served in diplomacy, although his older brother was at that time a temporary attaché to the

Berlin Embassy. Mondell had fallen in love with Rene, and believing everything he said, she had married him.

Criff had heard of this with mixed feelings.

He knew Rene remarkably well, and he was sure that her loyalties would not be divided when she was married. He might have been right in this had Sir Douglas, after his marriage, chosen to lead a life of righteousness. He had not so chosen. Three years brought them to the point of a legalised separation.

Mondell, who depended for his money on an elder relative who would undoubtedly have cut his allowance had matters gone to the length of a divorce was pleased enough to let it rest there.

As a consequence Rene, with time on her hands, looked round for something to do.

Stage work was hardly becoming for the wife of a baronet, and when Criff had approached her again she had willingly enough agreed to operate for him. At first her task had been simply to get information from wealthy industrialists in various countries, but it had slowly widened its scope. In the course of it, and with Criff's help, she had come to know by sight most of the agents of Department Z. Because other things had made it essential, she had learned a little of Criff's intentions in regard to them.

In short, that he looked on one or two as dangerous, and planned to remove them.

Criff had long foreseen the need for having complete control over her. There was only one way. Criff sent her to France on an unimportant job which he assured her was of vital importance. During the course of it a man had died violently. He had seen to it that circumstances pointed to Rene Mondel. Through his agents Criff had rescued her from a particularly nasty predicament, planning – should she show any inclination to desert him – to bring pressure to bear on the strength of this unsolved French crime.

Rene Mondell had a certain astuteness, but not a great deal of intelligence. If she was told exactly what to do and how to go about it, she could be an unqualified success, but if she had to start thinking seriously for herself, disaster was almost sure to follow. Gradually Criff's hold on her tightened until she honestly believed that she had to do what he told her.

Familiarity, even with violence, brought a measure of indifference towards it. Criff believed that she was too frightened to disobey an order. One day perhaps she would be too frightened even to obey, and then there would be an accident, but for the time being she was as fully in his confidence as anyone else – on the same level, in fact, as Shirin and von Hauf.

The measure of her fright could be judged from her manner when she had rushed into the flat with the news. She had her own flat in the same block, and there was no one to say she had visited Criff, unless the Department Z watchers had followed her. There was not the slightest reason to believe that they had.

No one had seen his two visitors, for they had come through the servants' doors.

Now, about to depart, Criff saw no danger.

'Excellent,' he said and not for the first time. 'von Hauf, you will go first – the back way. Shirin, you are better known in London, and you will go next. Should – yes, should anyone question you, say you have been with Lady Mondell! It is an excellent idea!'

Rene Mondell sat up sharply.

'It – '

'You will do exactly what you're told,' Criff said to Shirin. 'Should there be questions – even friendly questions – say that. Perhaps it would be a good idea to visit the all-night café, in Oxford Street. You might be followed, and asked questions. Rene, surely you have the good sense to realise that we must make absolutely sure that Shirin and I are not known to be associated?'

She frowned: Criff decided that it might be wiser to concede the point, for it was not of vital importance.

'All right – make use of it, Shirin, only in emergency. And tomorrow – there must be no more mistakes with Kerr. He is dangerous, I do not know of a man I fear more. Strike quickly, and the danger is over. Delay, and we may find ourselves in trouble. You understand, all of you?'

Shirin nodded. Von Hauf was by the door, and at a nod from Griff he pushed through, worried and trembling.

'Have you any ideas on how to deal with Kerr?' asked the Russian.

'Have *I*? That is your task, Shirin, and you surely have plenty of people to help you. Remember, use them *only* one at a time.' Criff chuckled as the door closed gently behind Gregaroff Shirin. But there was something animal in the sound. However, he was courtesy himself as he turned to Rene. 'And now, my dear, you must be tired. You have been a long time getting back from Surrey.'

Rene hesitated before she spoke.

'Yes. It wasn't pleasant. And of course I waited in the hope that Fencer would get away.' She had been at the White Star, Camberley, and had learned most of what she knew from local gossip – the story of the murdered Vallenan had travelled fast. 'I came straight back.'

Criff nodded, well-pleased.

'Now off to your flat and bed.'

She yawned, stretching gracefully with an unconscious voluptuousness that made Criff's eyes narrow. When he had first met her he had been sure that she followed the oldest profession of all, but for once he had made a mistake.

'All right. Adam – it's not dangerous, is it?'

Criff patted her shoulder.

'Just a little more care to be exercised, my dear, that's all. And I think in two weeks from now it will be finished. I shall not need to worry you again. Even that sad affair in Paris can be forgotten.'

Rene Mondell shivered, and hurried out. The weary-eyed valet, waiting in the next room until summoned, was told that he could go to bed. Criff decided to rest in an easy chair.

He had booked a passage for Poland on a plane leaving at noon, and he had several things to do in London first. He felt a little annoyed with himself for his momentary outburst of alarm. Rene was getting nervous, too nervous.

Lady Mondell certainly was: she was also getting wary, and wondering whether it was wise to let herself be ruled so completely by Adam Criff. It was a peculiar fact that she had hidden one vital thing from him. She had, in fact, lied when she had said that she had come straight back from Camberley.

Actually she had been to her own flat, two hours before she had visited Criff's, and before that she had spent an hour riding in a taxi with a man named Falling. Falling was a little younger than Rene Mondell, and somewhat unhappily in love with her. But he had, she knew, something to distract him, for he had started a few months before working for a man named Craigie and a Department called Z.

Rene Mondell had learned that when she had visited him once, to find Bob Kerr and Carruthers with him. But she had never disclosed this friendship to Adam Criff.

She hurried now along the warm passages, wondering what Criff would say if he knew she had kept the friendship secret: or what he would do.

She had been almost too eager that night to persuade Jim to leave England and go abroad for a year or two. Ostensibly because she was married, and he could never hope for her, actually because of her underlying fear that Criff would hurt him.

She fell asleep thinking of the cheerful blue eyes and the fair, curly hair of broad-shouldered, easy-speaking Jim Falling, that most recent member of Department Z. And ten minutes after she fell asleep, the telephone on Gordon Craigie's desk buzzed.

Craigie was alert in a moment. He lifted the receiver, and the man at the other end of the wire spoke quickly, spelling his name backwards, an introduction that was the ruling Department code.

'Craigie? G.N.I.L.L.A.F. speaking. All right?'

'Yes, Falling,' said the Chief of Department Z.

'Rene Mondell's just left Criff's flat – she's been there half-an-hour. Shirin, a Russian cove, came out ten minutes before her. No one seems to have seen him go in. Ashe, at the back, says a money-lender named von Hauf left that way. That's the lot.'

'Good work,' said Craigie.

He hesitated, for he fancied he detected an unusual note – almost one of reluctance – in the other man's voice. But Falling said nothing more, and Craigie told him to go off duty.

Falling, at a call-box at Marble Arch station, rang down and then walked slowly into the street.

He was frowning, and he felt like the very devil.

When he had first been told to keep an eye on Lady Mondell – not because of her association with Criff, but because she had been so frequently in foreign capitals at times which were difficult diplomatically, and Craigie's foreign agents had of course reported it – he had not imagined it would be much of a job. A bit of fooling with a blonde, and no more.

But Rene Mondell was not the usual type of blonde.

And Jim Falling was beginning to realise that he was really, not feignedly, in love with her. It was a devil of a business.

Had he been wise he would have told Craigie the truth, but he had not been able to bring himself to it.

As he reached his flat in Jermyn Street, a little man of the name of Platt hurried along the other side of the road. He had a lot to report next morning, to a certain gentleman who would telephone him.

Quite by chance, Platt had seen Rene Mondell with Falling, had followed them on their taxi ride, wondered what she was doing hob-nobbing with a man he had been told to watch carefully – in common with several other Department Z agents, for Criff was careful – and had hung around. She had spent an hour or so in her flat, come out for a breather, seen a couple more of the Z bozos around and scuttled in again. Maybe it was okay with the Boss, but maybe it wasn't.

Chapter 6

So Easy

At eleven o'clock next morning, after he had telephoned the man named Platt, Adam Criff discovered that Rene was playing a double game with him.

His first temptation was to confront her with it. On reflection, however, he believed he could twist this development to his advantage. It needed his personal attention, he decided, and he cancelled his Polish flight – thereby making Craigie ponder when the fact was discovered in the normal routine of Department Z.

While Craigie was trying to discover why Criff had suddenly changed his plans, and whether the man suspected that he was being watched, Criff was working out a new scheme. From the way he smiled from time to time it seemed as if it would be satisfactory. He even chuckled, and he sent out an order to Platt to get the man Falling, alive, and to take him to a small house in Essex bought and kept for such emergencies.

Criff, of course, did not know exactly what Falling had reported, but he saw the possibility that Shirin's visit had been discovered. He would have been less satisfied had he known that Department Z men were already making thorough inquiries about Shirin and von Hauf.

* * *

Meanwhile Mr Tino Platt was sitting in a small room in a large house in Harrow. The house was officially a private hotel, and at one time it had been a genuine concern. Later, however, Mr Adam Criff had bought it and a different management had taken over.

From that time onwards, dating practically from the time that M. Jules Doriennet had started to lose business, and English companies had been annoyed at receiving the wrong shipments of Vallenian goods, a peculiar type of guest had taken up residence at 18, Grattle Street, Harrow.

They were a mixed bunch. Some were well-educated, others practically illiterate. They apparently worked and rested in long stretches. A few, it was true, went out to work every day, but there were those who seemed to lounge about the house for weeks on end. The manager had let it be rumoured that he was building up a good connection with film 'extras' and that explanation satisfied the neighbours, as well as a tentative inquiry from the police.

Actually, of course, the various members of Criff's carefully organised English company lived there.

By chance Fencer had not stayed at Grattle Street, but at a different and genuine boarding house, as he had told Bob Kerr. But Mr. Platt did, and he had now received orders to 'bring in' the guy named Falling. He had been told by telephone that he could take two other men to help him.

Platt was uncertain whom to take, and he consulted the manager, a loose-limbed man named Jensen.

'Giddy and Jo,' said Jensen, as soon as the query was forthcoming. 'They know the ropes all right. You've gotta take him, you say, not push him over?'

'So de Essex place,' said Tino Platt. 'Dat's what de Boss ses.'

'Do what he says an' you won't come to no 'arm,' said Mr Jensen, and thus it was that two hours later Jim Falling – off duty for the day – had a visit from a tall, well-dressed man with an obviously professional manner.

Falling looked at his caller inquiringly.

'Lady Mondel asked me to come,' said the professional-looking gentleman with a disarming smile. 'If you could call at her flat sometime today, she would appreciate it. A slight accident – '

The professional-looking one, whose name was Giddy at

Grattle Street, Harrow, had a convincing manner, and yet he had some difficulty in keeping his elation from showing in his eyes. The young cove named Falling fell so easily.

Jim Falling watched the door close, stepped sharply to the window, and watched Giddy walk quickly along the street. He eyed the telephone longingly and then, with sudden decision, grabbed his hat and left his flat.

A comely maid admitted him to Lady Mondell's flat. It was smaller than Criff's, and less pretentiously furnished, though just as luxurious.

'How is she?' Falling asked sharply.

'She – she asked you to go straight in, sir.'

Falling nodded, and let the girl lead him to a bedroom door. At first only the foot of the bed was visible.

And then Jim Falling pulled himself up short, but he had no time to do anything. Just behind the door was the professional-looking Giddy. In one corner of the room, training a gun on Falling, was Tino Platt; and from the bed appeared the ungainly figure of a crook known as Flash Jo.

All three faces were split with grins at the ease of the catch. Falling made a sharp turn towards the hall, but Tino's gun moved and warned him that silence and stillness were advisable. Giddy closed the door, and slipped his right hand in his pocket.

'What the devil's this?' snapped Falling. 'Where's Lady Mondell?'

Giddy laughed.

'See what happens when young sparks like you fiddle around with married skirts, Mister Falling.'

'Cut it,' growled Tino Platt. 'Put de cosh on de guy, Giddy, we ain't got no time for shooting his mouth offen him.'

'Look here – ' began Falling.

He contrived one wild and useless swipe at the man named Jo, but the vicious swish of a cosh came first. Its leaded end cracked against Falling's head and he pitched forward into the waiting arms of Tino Platt.

'Say, would you believe it? So easy I reckon we oughta apologise, Giddy. Let's git de guy outside.'

It was not difficult for them to make it appear that Jim Falling was either drunk or ill. They reached the outside of the block of flats, and Flash Jo jumped to the door of a Daimler saloon that was standing there. Far more quickly than they had moved upstairs, they had Falling in the tonneau. Tino Platt joined him, Jo took the wheel, and Giddy watched the car drive off before turning towards the nearest telephone kiosk.

He saw, but did not specially notice, the battered-looking Austin 7 that rattled past in the wake of the Daimler. He did not see the driver of the Austin, five minutes later, lift two fingers towards a man at the wheel of a Frazer Nash car.

Bob Kerr, driving the Frazer Nash, saw the signal, and his eyes turned towards the Daimler. He followed it as far as the first fringes of Epping Forest. Then he pulled the Frazer Nash into the courtyard of the Swan Inn, and the Daimler – whose driver had noticed the smaller car and had started to wonder – grew more cheerful.

"'Okay, he's stopped,' he said to Tino.

'Sure,' said Tino.

Neither of them realised that as the Frazer Nash had gone off the trail, two other following cars had taken it up.

They had been summoned after a general police car call had been put out, via the man in the Austin 7, and had quickly reached the Daimler and the Frazer Nash, whose progress had been followed by every sharp-eyed policeman along the route.

Kerr was frowning, despite the ease of the chase.

It demonstrated the power and the thoroughness of Department Z as few other things could have done. Now they were working hard on the Doriennet-Criff affair, they were at fever-pitch, and the smooth co-operation with the police helped them. But Kerr was worried.

He thought back, to the hour before the chase had started.

It had been after the professional-looking Giddy had called on him that Jim Falling grew uneasy. He had not confided in Craigie, but now, at the eleventh hour, he decided to tell Kerr.

Kerr had told him how to act, but he had been worried about the youngster. Falling had blurted the whole thing out. His fondness for Lady Mondell, his belief that she returned his affection, the fact that he wished he had not started it. But Falling had guts. He was prepared to go as far as he could this time, even if he retired at the end of it.

Kerr wondered whether Falling would have the chance to retire.

If Criff was indeed the leader of the gang he had shown himself to be both brutal and unscrupulous. Kerr disliked the idea of sending a youngster to what might prove to be a nasty death. But – it was for the Department. They *had* to get further information on the strange happenings at Vallena, even at the price of a brave man's life.

As he waited for a message at the Swan, Kerr was thinking that at least six men he had known, grown friendly with, joked, eaten and worked with, had died in the past eighteen months; older, better, more valuable men than Falling, and all had died for the Department.

Some twenty minutes after he had pulled in, a policeman entered the saloon bar of the pub. He recognised Kerr at once and stepped towards him.

'Mr Kerr?'

Kerr nodded.

'I've just had a radio call, sir, asking you to go to Edge House, Elmswick.'

Kerr's eyes narrowed. So the others had traced the Daimler, and Falling was now at a house in Elmswick village, near Epping. The constable was able to give him explicit directions, and Kerr reached Edge House fifteen minutes after he had received the message.

Two other agents – who played a small part in the affair of Doriennet, and can be nameless – were waiting in the shadows of a copse of trees conveniently near. The house stood half a mile from the nearest house or habitation. Even in the hot glow of that September afternoon sun it managed to look dark, gloomy and sombre.

'Anyone gone in or out?' asked Kerr.

A fresh-faced young man said no. Kerr nodded, and gave instructions before walking boldly up the short drive of Edge House. There were times when direct approached was advisable and Kerr believed that this was one of them.

* * *

Jim Falling did not know whether to be pleased with or sorry for himself. The call from the man styling himself a doctor had convinced him it was essential to confide in someone. He had chosen Kerr, for there had always been something about the ex-flying ace that instilled confidence. Kerr had told him exactly what to do, but had also reminded him of the dangers of the game. There were many.

'I'll take them,' Falling had said with a quick smile.

Now, conscious and with a badly aching head, he was sitting on a couch in an upstairs room of a house that seemed as far as possible away from civilisation. Opposite him stood Tino Platt.

Falling, his hands and feet bound tightly, licked his dry lips.

'Who's the swine who's paying you for this?'

'Now ain't that too bad?' drawled Tino. 'He wants to know who de Boss is! Maybe he'll tell you.'

Tino, whose mentality was of the type to appreciate the humour of playing with a helpless victim, broke off as there came the sudden, strident ringing of a telephone bell. Seeing that the house had been unoccupied when they had arrived, it was something of a surprise. Tino stepped back, shut the door, and hurried downstairs. Flash Jo was holding the receiver in his hand as he stood in the small, gloomy hallway.

'It's him, Tino.'

'De Boss? Reckon he's aimin' t'know whether we got de guy,' said Tino. As the voice of the Boss came sharply over the line, Tino's complacency disappeared.

'You were followed,' said Criff. 'Put him away, and get off yourself. And move quickly.'

Tino Platt swung from the telephone towards Flash Jo.

'Get de car out an' make it hum. Dere's trailers on us.'

'*What!*' Jo's startled face turned pale. He hurried towards the garage, while Tino Platt raced up the stairs towards Falling's door.

He flung it open with his left hand, and snatched his automatic from his right-shoulder holster. Falling, who had been trying desperately to loosen the cords, saw that red face twisted in savage anger, and was suddenly, dreadfully afraid. Pictures of Kerr, Rene, Craigie and a dozen others flashed through his mind, as Platt flicked the gun.

And then Falling drew himself up, with a queer dignity. He *knew* what was coming. His lips were steady as Tino's fingers tightened and relaxed, three times. The first bullet did its work. Falling sagged forward. Death had at least been instantaneous for the youngest member of Department Z.

Tino reached the hall as the car with Flash Jo at the wheel drew up. Tino jumped towards it. He had been through stick-ups before, and he had never failed to shoot himself out. He reckoned that anyone who followed him would not dream he would shoot on sight.

As the car moved off Bob Kerr was opening the drive gate. The bend in the drive hid the oncoming car from sight, but Kerr heard the engine and drew a little to one side. Tino Platt, his eyes narrowed, waited and watched, gun in hand.

Chapter 7

Kerr Takes It Hard

Kerr had no idea that Falling had been murdered in cold blood. He had no idea that the men in the oncoming car were prepared to shoot on sight, but he had a memory of what had happened on the previous day. His face was quite expressionless as the Daimler turned the bend.

He saw Jo, and he saw Tino. It was enough. Moving faster than it seemed possible a man could move, he reached the shelter of the trees, and as he did so bullets sprayed about him. They spattered on the trees and in the grass, one tugged at Kerr's coat sleeve as he levelled his gun. He fired three times, at the wheels and not the men.

He saw the car rock, heard the explosion. Flash Jo bent over the wheel in a desperate endeavour to gain control. At the same time the two Department men who had gone towards the rear of the house broke cover.

But Kerr hardly needed them.

He knew now that Falling was dead, and he was filled with a cold determination to avenge him.

Tino Platt, his eyes blazing, fired his last shot, and then opened the car door to run for it. Kerr's bullet struck him in the chest and he dropped half-in, half-out of the car.

Even Kerr shuddered.

Jo, aiming to travel on the wheel rims, urged the car forward. It ploughed on, dragging Tino's body with it.

And Jo suddenly realised that all hope of escape was over.

Kerr left him to the two Department men and then started to run towards the house. Three minutes afterwards he pushed open the door of the second floor room where

Falling was lying. He stood very still on the threshold. Then swore, coldly and slowly.

* * *

Mr. Adam Criff, millionaire-adventurer grown rich on wars, was sitting in his easiest chair, and scowling. There was little of the debonair man-about-town in his expression. He was waiting for the telephone to ring, with a message from Platt.

Criff was definitely uneasy. If his plans had misfired, was it possible to trace their origin back to himself?

He thought not, he hoped not, but he could not be absolutely sure. Tino and Jo might talk of Grattle Street, and although no one there knew of Criff's part in the affair, the police might be able to trace the telephone calls, usually made from Criff's nearest call-box. Moreover Criff had given them a number, so that they could call him back. It was not in the directory, but the police would have access to private numbers.

Criff was beginning to sweat.

He had sent Rene Mondell over to Paris, to make sure she was out of the way while he dealt with Falling.

But Falling was dead.

Criff wished fervently that he had not given those last instructions. His personal inclination had over-ridden his caution.

That was not all. There was something else which was worrying Adam Criff.

He had always disliked admitting it, but he was not the top dog. There were those above him whose orders he had to obey. He knew of them only vaguely. He himself had heard nothing from them that day, but he had learned that both von Hauf and Shirin had left England hurriedly, obviously ordered to do so by that higher command. It worried and harassed him. It was rare that he did not have the order to give to the others, and it suggested that the higher command was beginning to lose faith in Adam Criff.

Well, his suitcase was packed. He had a private plane waiting for him in a private airfield, and he did not think anyone knew of its whereabouts. At the first real rumour of trouble, Criff would be away.

He heard the ring of the door bell, and started.

His man's footsteps were deadened by a thick carpet, but he heard the murmur of voices, and then silence.

The door opened, and for the first time Criff and Kerr met face to face.

Criff was so shocked that he could only stare, his mouth agape and his eyes widening with alarm. Kerr saw guilt and fear on that handsome face with the too-red, too-full lips, and Kerr remembered Falling's hanging head, the three bullets buried in Falling's body. He closed the door slowly, without speaking.

Criff tried to speak and could not.

He felt a surge of fear that he had never known before, and his tongue clove to the roof of his mouth. Kerr's silence was uncanny. That wooden, forceful face. Those grey eyes, neither narrowed nor widened, but deadly. Criff was beginning to tremble, the tension was unbearable.

His voice came, harsh with useless anger.

'Who are you, and what do you mean by coming here, what – '

Kerr said stonily: 'Tell me, Criff, would you prefer to be imprisoned for life, or to be shot – three times – and see death coming?'

Criff was half-mad now, with a dreadful fear. Kerr *knew*.

'You – you're talking nonsense, I don't know what – ' His hands were trembling as he moved them towards his pocket. There was a gun there, a small automatic. If he could just reach it –

Kerr went on: 'You're a murdering swine, Criff. Falling was killed on your orders, I'm lucky to have escaped. You killed Doriennet and you've probably killed others. I could forgive you but for Falling.'

Criff's hand was in his pocket. He could feel the cold steel of the gun, but his fingers were trembling too much to find the trigger.

'We caught two of your men, we've unearthed Grattle Street, and we've found that it was *you* who phoned the orders.'

Criff had the gun ready and was actually fingering the trigger. But Kerr was no longer standing in front of him; he had moved towards the window. His hand slipped in and out of his pocket like lighting. There was the slightest of smiles on his face.

Criff felt the bullet bite through the fleshy part of his right arm. Kerr's gun was still trained on him, glinting as coldly as his eyes. 'I wanted you to try for a gun, Criff, it gave me an excellent chance of making you know what it's like to be shot at. Now – start talking. If you don't the next shot will be fatal.'

Criff's jaws were working. The man meant it. That dreadful, frightening stare, that harsh clipped voice.

'You – you daren't! It's murder, you can't do it, you –'

'It would be self-defence,' said Kerr quietly. 'Understand? Your gun's in your pocket, and you fired through the coat. Self-defence, Criff! You saw me lock the door – and I'll tell you that one or two of my men are waiting outside. There's no hope for you, unless you talk.'

Criff, a pain in his shoulder that was like a living fire, felt dreadfully afraid. It would be useless to attempt to bluff this man. He had heard stories of Kerr, he had been told that Kerr was the one man in Craigie's Department who was really dangerous, who stopped at *nothing* to get what he wanted. He had given orders – after receiving them from that higher command – to have Kerr killed.

Kerr breathed slowly as he stepped towards the millionaire.

'Listen. I know what orders were given to Doriennet. I know that *you* are partly responsible for the wrong shipments from Vallena to England. I know that you arranged for Falling to die, for me to die, and I guess that you killed

Doriennet. Fencer may have fired the shot, but you killed him. What I don't know is *why* it's happening, but I'm going to find out. If I have to kill you by inches, I'm going to.'

He slapped the cringing man sharply across the face, and Criff's shriek was stifled in his throat.

'I – I don't know, I – '

Kerr shot out his right hand again, and it was more than a slap this time. Criff suddenly realised what was meant by stopping at *nothing*.

'You don't know, eh? That's unfortunate for you, Criff. Because I think you do, and I'm going to find out.'

He was serious, of course.

He knew that he had to find out what Criff knew. He had a deepest conviction that behind the absurd fiddling with small shipments of goods that Doriennet had talked about there was something far bigger, far more dangerous. He knew that England was concerned, and he wanted to know why.

He *had* to know why. It was his job.

He shot his right hand out suddenly, and grabbed Criff's uninjured left wrist. Criff started to shriek, and then the pain that sheered through his body became agonising.

'All right – all right! I'll tell you!'

Kerr released his hold, stood over the millionaire, and nodded. He felt relieved, for it had been easier than he had expected. Kerr did not always like the things he had to do, even with a man like Criff, who was now at such a peak of terror and pain that it did not occur to him to lie. Kerr knew that. But as he listened he experienced an overwhelming disappointment, *because Criff did not know a great deal*!

'Kerr – Kerr – I'm only one. Only one! I get orders – from abroad. Several – countries. The trick with the Vallena stuff was – '

Kerr heard him out. He felt sure that Criff was telling everything he knew, and the sense of disappointment was greater than ever when the millionaire, gasping, pain-wracked and terror-stricken, finished and flopped back in his chair. Kerr felt a sudden pity for the man. He turned round, found the whisky and poured out a strong measure. Criff had hardly the strength to lift it to his lips, but Kerr left him to it and went to the door. He had finished with Criff for the time being, and Carruthers and Davidson – those two stalwarts were in the next room – could carry on.

Kerr opened the door.

He opened it slowly, by habit, and what he saw was like a blow in the face.

He caught a glimpse of Wally Davidson stretched out on the carpet, and there was blood coming from Davidson's neck. As his eyes took in the picture he saw also the man who was standing in the window recess of the first room, holding something that looked like a black tennis ball in his hand.

Kerr saw him very clearly.

He was abnormally tall – six-feet-and- a-half at least – and he lobbed the tennis ball towards the doorway. But he lobbed it a fraction of a second too late to be really effective.

As the bomb crashed against the woodwork, Kerr jumped backwards and slammed the door shut. The explosion shook the walls of the flat, set the pictures rattling, and smashed the windows, but it did no more than knock Kerr breathless. He was alert enough to find his gun and stay on the floor, the gun trained towards the door.

It was smashed inwards. Through the smoke and flame he saw the far door close, and the tall man disappear, and he swore as he jumped up.

A moment later he dropped down again.

Something had gone wrong with his right foot: it would not hold him. Kerr grimaced as he dragged himself up slowly.

Flame had started to run along the walls of the room beyond. They were running far too fast for it to be the result of the bomb, and Kerr could even see the trickle of oil as yet untouched by the flames. Davidson, Carruthers and the servant Jones were in that room, a room that would be an inferno in less than five minutes.

Kerr grabbed the telephone and pushed it towards Criff. 'Phone the fire-brigade,' he snapped. 'Give the fire-alarm.'

He paused long enough to take the gun out of Criff's pocket, and then started to hobble towards the door. The heat of the flames in the room beyond was already overpowering, and his face was bleak as he reached it.

Davidson and Carruthers were both stretched out, both knifed. They might be dead or alive. The servant –

'Gone,' muttered Kerr, hardly knowing what he was saying or doing as he reached Carruthers – nearer that creeping fire than Davidson. 'One of – them, of course. One of – for God's sake, Carry, don't act the fool!'

Kerr knew he was perilously near delirium; the shock of the explosion had been more than he had realised. He hoped to God that Criff had called the fire brigade. Painfully, tenaciously, he lugged Carruthers towards the door of Criff's room.

Then back for Davidson, with the smoke choking him and the flames singing his hair.

Thank God he was alive: his eyes flickered open.

'Crawl – for the door,' gasped Kerr.

Davidson had strength enough. Kerr, sweating, gasping, almost crying, managed to lug Carruthers into Criff's room. Davidson, on his hands and knees, and with a horrible crescent of red round his throat, reached the door and collapsed against it.

Kerr saw that Criff, still sitting with the telephone in front of him, was staring ahead of him blankly. The telephone receiver was in his right hand, and it did not move.

Criff was dead!

Kerr stared at him stupidly, seeing the bullet hole in the side of his neck. Shot through the open window, he decided. As in a daze he heard the crackling in the microphone, and lifted the receiver.

A girl's voice came sharply to his ears.

'What is it – what's the trouble there?'

'Fire,' Kerr gasped. 'Fire – and police! Superintendent – Miller. Fire – fire – fire – '

His head was whirling, his pulse hammering. Smoke, shock and the excruciating pain of his ankle combined to beat him. He stood shouting fire like a madman, he had a moment's sanity while he remembered that no one would be able to get in by the door, and as he moved towards the window he staggered, sprawling forward, blind and helpless.

Behind, the fire roared and crackled more loudly as it crept along the carpet from the next room, slow, menacing, ravenous.

* * *

Superintendent Horace Miller, of Scotland Yard, was a stolid representative of all that was best in the C.I.D. He rarely grew excited, as rarely angry.

On that September afternoon he was sitting in his office and frowning. Frowning because he had just been warned by the Chief Commissioner, Sir William Fellowes, that he was to stand by to help Craigie and Department Z. It was a normal occurrence for him, which explained the fact that his life was considerably more exciting and his work more dangerous than that of a shrewd, self-made Superintendent's should have been.

He knew, of course, about the Doriennet affair, but he had been in the north country on a poison case, and had only arrived back two hours ago. He had hoped for three or four days easy going, but nothing was ever easy going with the Department.

The telephone rang, and Miller mechanically stretched out a hand and lifted the receiver.

'This is the Mayfair Exchange, Superintendent. We have just had a call of fire from 191, Devenett Court. A man who did not give his name asked us to advise you . . . Yes, the fire-brigade has been informed.'

'Thanks.' Miller banged the receiver down and leapt for

his hat, issuing a sharp order for a sergeant to accompany him.

Three or four minutes later Miller's large Singer moved off. As it neared Devenett Court, smoke was already pouring from the windows. Miller swore as he saw the crowd, braked and jumped out, running as fast as his sixteen stone could take him. He did not know who had sent that message, but this was Criff's address, and it would certainly have been one of the Department men.

And Good God, if that fire had a hold –

Chapter 8

Criffs' Story

Miller recognised the Captain in charge of the fire brigade which was working desperately to keep the flames from spreading to the adjoining flats. Two more of these at least were doomed, and the occupants had been moved out quickly, their furniture pushed anywhere until the danger was past. The crowd was surging with excitement as first smoke then fire billowed out of the window, the streams of hissing water seeming only to add to the confusion.

Miller, pushing his way towards Webb – the Brigade captain – saw an escape was up against one window. He glimpsed a helmet, caught by the sun. Over the man's shoulder was a limp body.

Miller, his heart thumping, grabbed Webb's arm.

The Brigade captain swung round angrily.

'Get to blazes – oh! Sorry, Miller, I thought it was some blasted reporter. Nasty show.'

'Anyone down yet?'

Webb, middle-aged, grizzled and sceptical, grinned.

'One – but he's dead. A job for you, because he wasn't burned to death. Over there – and by God!' exclaimed Webb with a thunderous roar. 'There's that blasted reporter pestering them again!'

The captain stretched out to grip the shoulder of a small, round-faced man, whose scowling pugnaciousness would have amused Miller at a different moment.

'Listen, I've told you twice to keep off. Damn it, you're like a bloody jackal – clear off!'

Miller looked on with a certain degree of sympathy. Newspapermen were one of the worries of his life. But it was a job, and it had to be done. The main trouble was deciding how far to let them go.

Then he reached the outstretched body.

'Good Lord!' exclaimed Miller. 'Criff!'

With growing tension Miller saw the bullet mark in the neck, and the bloodstains on the singed coat and shirt.

Webb, still grumbling about young cubs, glanced at him inquiringly.

'Know him?'

'Do I know him? murmured Horace Miller, as though he had been asked whether he would recognise the King. 'Yes, I do. No one else down yet?'

'Only those by the escape.'

Miller pushed his way back again. Police, firemen, the flat tenants – those intimately touched by the fire – the staff of the office building also affected and a few Press men, made up the crush. Miller was sweating and cursing by the time he reached the foot of the escape.

A billow of smoke came down on him, making him choke. Water was coming down the walls like a miniature Niagara, but Miller, drenched though he was, did not budge.

For he recognised the two outstretched men.

Kerr, Bob Kerr, and Davidson. Oh, God, *they'd* caught it. Craigie's best men, and – and Davidson's throat was cut.

He pushed forward, and a fireman stopped him roughly.

'Say, you –'

'Miller, of the Yard,' said Miller brusquely.

The fireman nodded and apologised. A fresh roar, telling of another start from the burning room, was echoing in Miller's ears as he bent over Kerr. He could see that the chief agent was still breathing, but he was feverishly anxious to know what the doctor thought.

A medico was already looking at Davidson.

'Well?' Miller snapped.

'Bad, I'm afraid. Not much damage by the fire, but that –'

He pointed to the vicious ring of dried blood encircling Davidson's throat. Miller turned sharply away, almost cannoning into the two firemen carrying another unconscious figure.

A moment later he recognised Bob Carruthers, his fair hair falling in singed wisps. Kerr – Davidson – Carruthers. Craigie's three most lively agents. How many more?

Miller felt a hand clutch at his sleeve, and swung round, to see Lois Dacre's set face.

Knowing something of the way things were between her and Bob Kerr, he forced a smile.

'He's all right, Miss Dacre.'

Lois looked darkly about her, her lips set very tightly.

'Any idea what happened?'

'None at all' said Miller. 'How did you get on the scene?'

'I know Bob had come to see – to see Criff.'

'Hmm. Looks as though there was a shindy up there all right, and Criff's johnnies made it,' Miller said thoughtfully. 'I – well I'm damned!'

He saw the persistent cub of a reporter tapping the doctor's shoulder, and he deserted Lois quickly. The girl watched him, as the cub turned tail and slipped away.

'Jackals, Webb called 'em, and he wasn't far wrong,' growled Miller. 'Well, there's not much we can do. Does Craigie know?'

'Yes, I've just phoned him.'

'Good girl,' said Miller, his voice approving, yet slightly patronising. He had found it hard to believe that Gordon Craigie was trusting a girl to work for him – Lois Dacre was the first woman agent of Department Z. 'What's it all about?

'I don't know,' said Lois bitterly. 'I wish to goodness I could discover someone – something. It's just standing here that does the damage, and – well!'

She broke off, glanced down at Bob Kerr, then nodded to Miller.

'Tell Craigie I've gone after the woman in the case, will you?' she said, and with another sharp, unamused smile, she slipped through the crowd. Miller pushed his hat to the back of his head. She was a cool 'un, a proper partner for Kerr. But –

The medico, brusque, alert, plump and short-tempered, glared at him.

'This man' – he pointed to Kerr – 'should be all right in a day or two. The others are touch and go. The ambulances should be along soon. They've to go to Marion's Hospital.'

Miller nodded, thanked him, and set out to find Webb. The fire, which had threatened to be really dangerous, was now under control. Already the flames had stopped coming out of the window, and the smoke cloud was lessening.

After a struggle Miller managed to reach Captain Webb's elbow. He turned promptly.

'Petrol. Not a shred of doubt about it. My goodness, Miller, you've got something on your hands here!'

'You're telling me,' said Miller heavily. He moved into the building and came face to face with a tall, thin, hatchet-faced man wearing a dark grey suit and a somewhat battered hat. It was Gordon Craigie, head of Department Z.

'Hallo, Craigie.'

'Eh? Oh, hallo, Miller. Bad business.'

'Heard about the others?'

'Tell me.'

Miller told what he could, and Craigie listened, a slight frown wrinkling his forehead.

'Hmm. Well, I suppose we have to expect it. Criff was shot dead, you say?'

'Looks as though Kerr or one of the others got him.'

Craigie's eyes twinkled. He had so trained himself to show nothing of his thoughts, depressing or otherwise, that he seemed always to be in exactly the same frame of mind – a good-tempered and patient one.

'Does it? I can't imagine those three and Criff together ending that way.'

'Well, you know them best. By the way, I've just seen Miss Dacre. She says she's after a woman.'

'A woman, eh? Hm. That'll be Lady Mondell – but of

course you haven't heard about it yet. Come round in' – he glanced at his watch – 'three hours, will you? You might ask the Commissioner if he can spare me half-an-hour at the same time.'

Miller promised that he would, and Craigie walked along to the scene of the fire. But Webb assured him there wasn't a chance of finding anything in the flat, apart from the traces of arson – and there was not the slightest doubt about that.

Craigie nodded soberly.

'Thanks – it's what I wanted to know.'

He left the captain, to find the crowd thinning outside, three people leaving the scene for every one who came towards it. Craigie smiled sardonically. The old, old curiosity, and the old ignorance. If he were to tell them that the men concerned risked their lives as secret service agents, they would assume at once that they were acting for a film company.

Did it matter?

Craigie did not think so. He called a cab ordering the driver to go to Marion's Hospital. Kerr had been to see him, only an hour and a half back.

The chief agent had reported the affair at Edge House, had explained his conclusions, and had been grim-voiced and gloomy despite the fact that Flash Jo had talked of Grattle Street.

It had taken Craigie five minutes to prove that the telephone number which Flash Jo and others called from 18, Grattle Street was Adam Criff's. Kerr had more than guessed it.

'But supposing Criff doesn't know much, and there's someone else? Do we leave him?' he had asked Craigie.

Craigie had shaken his head.

'Can't afford it with a man like Criff, Bob. See what you can force out of him, and then bring him here. Better take Wally, and perhaps Bob Carruthers with you. Need anyone else?'

'That should be enough.'

Craigie had decided that it would be. Now he knew he had made a mistake. And that was the trouble, of course. He was always making mistakes, he had to make them. He wished to God he was infallible, that Kerr was, and the others.

That particular trio were strong enough to take care of any normal show. Whatever had happened had been very much out of the ordinary.

Had Criff talked? Craigic ached to know.

And there was another thing: Lois Dacre. He wished she had not gone off on her own, though had it been one of the men he would not have thought twice about it. Odd how he could not get into the habit of relying on Lois, although she had shown resource equal if not superior to any of the men.

'Here you are, sir.'

Craigie jumped out, paid the cabby, and went into the hospital. He knew the house-surgeon, and there would be no need to show an identity card.

The surgeon, Sir Wilfrid Mayer, tall, bluff, keen-eyed, greeted him amiably.

'Hallo, Craigie. After those fire victims, eh?'

'And in a hurry, Mayer,' said Craigie.

'As usual, eh? Well, I wish I could say for sure about the two big fellows. Nasty throat wounds. The other fellow will pull round. Conscious ten minutes ago, and demanding to see you. I'll take you up.'

Kerr was in a private ward. He was heavily bandaged, his right foot making a formidable mound under the bed-clothes, but he was obviously desperately anxious to talk.

He greeted Craigie with feverish relief.

'Thank God you've come, I thought the idiots would never fetch you. Listen, Gordon – Criff was shot through a window. That man Kryn chucked a grenade, and set fire to the place – yes, I saw him with my own eyes. Kryn's our man for the time being. I don't know how Wally and Carry were put out, but the servant was missing, so it looks as if it was his doing.'

Craigie leaned forward.

'Did Criff talk?'

Kerr grimaced.

'As much as he could. He didn't know a great deal, although he must have known enough to make the others want to kill him.'

Craigie pulled nervously at his lower lip.

'So there are others, eh?'

'I don't think there's any doubt about it. Everything pointed a damned sight too easily to Criff.'

'*Too* easily?'

'It looks to me – hindsight of course – as though the swabs *wanted* him to catch a packet.' Kerr wiped his forehead. 'Listen, old man, Criff was *always* in the limelight. It worried me. A man really behind the scenes wouldn't show himself as much as Criff did. It's obvious now that he was told to. Criff held the limelight while the others collected the cash.'

'And who are the others?' asked Craigie.

Kerr was silent for a moment, his shallow breathing coming too quickly. He had put a great deal into this effort. Too much. He cursed his own weakness, but managed to gather enough strength to say slowly:

'I don't know. Criff *always* meets them in Vallena. He named Prell, the Vallenian Foreign Secretary as one of them, and said he didn't know the names of the others. When he saw them they were always disguised.

'Sigmund Prell, eh?'

'That's the fellow. Well – these orders for putting the wrong goods in English shipments. A simple explanation, Craigie. So simple we didn't think of it.'

Kerr heaved himself up on one elbow.

'And damnably cunning. By doing it, they made English firms take their business elsewhere. At the moment we are buying practically nothing from Vallena. That gives the Vallenian Government every reason for putting a hell of a high tariff on our goods – *and* for breaking off economic relationship. And Craigie: practically *all* our stuff for south Russia, northern Rumania and southern Poland is shipped via Vallena. Supposing Vallena, annoyed because we don't buy from them, put up exorbitant rates? We've got to pay, or send goods via longer and more expensive routes. It's an almighty stab at our mid-European trade. And that – ' Kerr managed a smile – 'is about as far as I can think. My head's aching like the very devil, damn it.'

Craigie stood up abruptly. It was the first time he had ever heard Bob Kerr breathe a word of complaint. If he was not careful he would put Kerr back for days, and he was going to need him badly.

'Sorry, old man. You've worked it out pretty tightly, and I'll follow up. The whole crowd is either scotched or has cleared out of England, that's pretty certain, so you're all right for a few days.'

Kerr nodded, but Craigie knew he had not really heard his words.

* * *

The Chief of Department Z left the hospital, after learning that there was no change in the serious condition of his other two agents. He knew that Kryn was still in England, but he had tried to ease Kerr's mind.

So it *looked* like an effort to block British goods from reaching some of the mid-European countries. That was something to work on, anyhow. It would go deeper, of course. The amount of trade was not tremendous. Big, of course, and serious if the British manufacturers lost it.

Craigie reached the steps of the hospital, and heard the usual roar of traffic, the usual hum of conversation and the bellowing of frenzied-voiced newspaper sellers.

Craigie bought a paper and opened it out. He frowned when he read under a headline that the beautiful Princess Katrina of Vallena was planning a solo-flight to Africa.

Then he stood dead still, quite unaware of the jostling

crowd around him. He hardly noticed them: he saw only the stop-press message.

> Sigmund Prell Vallenian Foreign
> Secretary reported assassinated
> by unidentified Russian agent –
> A.1. News Exchange.

Prell! The only man Criff had been able to identify.

Chapter 9

Old Friends

It was one of the rare occasions when Gordon Craigie was shaken out of his acquired calm. With waving arms he called peremptorily for a taxi, and jumped in.

So Prell had been murdered.

Craigie knew that it was another step, and a longer one, than the others. It suggested that things were moving to a head, for no one would arrange the assassination of a prominent diplomat unless there was an urgent reason for it.

The ruthlessness of it appalled him.

He was also at a loss. Whereas before they had known something of Criff and had slowly discovered others, now they were absolutely in the dark. Unless one of the men apprehended at Grattle Street could give information, the three slim chances lay in finding:

(a) The tall man named Kryn, sometimes known as Jacobs.
(b) Von Hauf, a German Jew.
(c) Shirin, a White Russian.

Until that morning Kryn had been at the Riltaz Hotel. Craigie was wondering why the agents following him had not stopped him from doing damage at Devennet Court. Obviously he had given his watchers the slip, visited Criff, discovered Kerr there (perhaps he had already learned of the coup at Grattle Street) and acted accordingly. The disappearance of Jones, the butler-valet, suggested that Criff himself had been served by a man spying for that high command which had always worried Criff, and was now beginning to worry Craigie.

Kerr's rough sketch of the possibilities was precious near the truth, Craigie thought.

Criff *had* always been too much in evidence. Had he been directing things himself he would have been far more circumspect. It was true that Craigie had wondered at times why the man had been so much in the limelight but he had decided that it was a form of vanity bolstered up by confidence in his immunity from trouble. Craigie was now telling himself he had made another mistake.

Mistake – mistakes! His head whirled with them, his heart was sick because of them. And here he was, with three of his best agents *hors de combat*, with young Falling dead, with the people he did know of on the opposite side dead or missing, and an unpleasant feeling that the big trouble which he had feared, was looming near.

But supposing Vallena, because of the refusal of English merchants to buy Vallenian goods, did put up a vicious tariff? Supposing they did push up freight charges, making the market extremely difficult for England: who would benefit?

Craigie began to feel a little more satisfied.

The reason why the blockade of British goods was wanted, always assuming Kerr had been right, was that someone else would get the trade. That someone would benefit considerably. Say a twentieth of British trade was lost: a small proportion looked at like that, but some tens – no, hundreds – of millions a year. Now the plot was taking on the shape of an international trade racket.

The cab jerked to avoid another coming behind it, and Craigie glanced into the interior of the cab. He saw a shortish, pug-faced man who was glaring ahead of him. Craigie did not recognise him, though Captain Webb and Superintendent Miller would certainly have done so.

Nevertheless it occurred to Craigie then that he was being damned careless. For many years he had managed his work in such secrecy that very few people had associated him with the Intelligence. But now he was better known, and as likely a victim of a bullet as Kerr or any of the others. Craigie's lips drooped in the somewhat mournful smile that characterised him. He often wondered whether he was as important and as effective as he believed. While he was working it seemed impossible that anyone else could replace him. Supposing someone did shoot him, here and now, what substantial difference would it make to – for instance – the Vallenian affair?

None, thought Gordon Craigie.

It might hold up the game for a while, and the other side would progress a little faster, but someone – the Chief Commissioner, Kerr, one of a dozen permanent officials from the Foreign Office – would take over. And on it would go as smoothly and effectively as before.

An hour and a half had passed since he had left Miller, and it was now two o'clock. Time to eat, thought Craigie with some surprise, and before long Miller and Fellowes would be coming to see him.

'Scotland Yard, sir.' The cabby pushed back the sliding glass partition.

'Make it the Foreign Office,' Craigie said.

'Right you are, sir.'

Craigie was deposited at the Foreign Office. A few yards ahead of him a taxi slowed down, just long enough for the pug-faced man believed by some to be a newspaper reporter, to look out of the rear window of the cab.

As he did so, Pug Face fingered an automatic in his pocket.

There was Craigie, the mainspring of British Intelligence, walking briskly along the pavement towards a small door leading to the Foreign Office. There was a man who worked for Mr Kryn, sitting in a perfect position for shooting Craigie in the back. Craigie was within a fraction of a second of death as he walked unknowingly onwards.

Pug Face glanced at the traffic about him. His driver was a good man, and would get away if anyone could. But there still remained a damnable risk of being caught.

Had he been Tino Platt or Fencer, Craigie would have been dead in that moment. As it was Pug Face hesitated long enough for Craigie's right foot to disappear into the doorway. Then the man raised his gun – and Craigie disappeared altogether.

'Too late, damn it!' muttered Pug Face to himself.

He felt relieved, not because he had avoided killing a man, but because he had avoided the possibility of being caught. Craigie had been too quick for him, a lucky thing for Craigie and perhaps himself.

Pug Face tapped on the glass partition.

'Strand Hotel, driver.'

'Right, sir.' Driver and Pug Face had worked together in their mysterious ways for a long time, but in all things they appeared to be strangers. The cab moved from the kerb about the time that Craigie entered the office of the Foreign Secretary, and was lost in the traffic.

There had recently been changes in the Cabinet, and the late Foreign Secretary, one Campion, had been pushed to a less onerous job, while a younger though still middle-aged man had replaced him. Mr Miles Bettin possessed guts, a good appearance, a vitriolic tongue that would sooner or later get him into trouble with the back-benchers, and – to Craigie the most unlikely attribute of a Foreign Secretary – he knew what he wanted and always tried to get it.

'Hallo, Craigie, I've been expecting you.' Bettin smiled, buttoning a perfectly cut coat about a perfectly trim torso. 'Or perhaps I should say I expected you to send for me. Comes to a pretty pass when you only have to press a bell, and there we are!'

Craigie nodded and smiled fleetingly.

'What's this about Prell?'

'I've just been dictating orders for the Baj embassy,' said Bettin. 'A bad business.' He fiddled with a small flower in his buttonhole. 'Killed by an Ogpu agent they say. No real proof yet, and of course Moscow denies it. Anyhow, Prell is dead enough. Shot as he walked from his home to the office.'

Bettin palmed his sleek hair, which was beginning to grey a little at the temples. His lips were pursed; his eyes, grey and shrewd, were narrowed as he regarded Craigie.

'What's the murderer's name?' asked Craigie.

'Vonovitch. Stefan Vonovitch.'

'Oh-ho! An Ogpu agent right enough, or he was up to three months ago. One of their stars. But it doesn't fit in.'

Bettin pushed cigarettes across his desk.

'I thought you'd have something to say. What doesn't it fit in with?'

'I won't smoke, thanks. The way thing are going. They're not running too well. You had my report this morning about Criff, and the Vallenian business?'

'The Doriennet murder? Yes.'

'Well, Criff's dead. He talked a little, and then was shot by someone working – at one time – with him. It makes things awkward. But what makes it more interesting from our point of view is that Criff implicated Prell, before he died.'

Bettin stared hard at his visitor.

'Implicated *Prell*?'

'What time was he shot?' asked Craigie.

'Greenwich mean time, about twelve-forty-five.'

'As late as that, eh? Twelve-forty-five. I had word about the fire at Devennet Court at – when was it? – near enough twelve o'clock. Say Criff was shot, after he had talked, at about eleven forty-five. So they *could* have discovered that he'd given Prell away, called Baj and arranged for Prell to be killed because he was the obvious man we should go after.' Craigie was looking paler than usual. 'I don't like this, Bettin. It looks now as though Prell was killed because Criff talked. It makes the whole show a damned sight more far-reaching, and a lot more complicated.'

Craigie went on to give the Foreign Secretary a resumé of the affair to date. The Foreign Secretary took it quietly but it was difficult to say which of the two men seemed more worried when Craigie finally left the office. It was a quarter to three, and Craigie sent a messenger for sandwiches and made himself some coffee before he sat back and tried to work the thing out. Fellowes and Miller would be along at half-past three, and the Yard might, by now, have discovered something about the fire at Devennet Court. Might, for instance, have located Jones, Kryn or anyone else connected.

But it was not likely.

Three of his five telephones were humming when he entered the office, and he took each receiver off, telling the men at the other end to hold on. Then he started to take the reports, pencil and notebook in hand.

Agent 39 reported that he and Agent 25 had lost Kryn. The man had left the Riltaz Hotel, and dodged them at Piccadilly. Before that he had been visited by a short man, youngish-looking, officially named Brown, and possessed of a pug face.

'Ever seen him before?' asked Craigie.

'No – a new one on me.'

'All right,' said Craigie. 'I'll phone you a bit later.'

He did not tell him what had happened since Kryn had evaded him. What was the use of worrying him, making him feel that in some measure at least he was responsible for the mess at Devennet Court? Craigie rarely blamed an agent for a mistake or a failure.

Agent 6, or Dodo Trale, that immaculate and laconic young man who was the oldest agent on Craigie's books in years of service, came next. Trale had been visiting Grattle Street, Harrow.

'None of them know much, Gordon. We got all the information we can from them. One fellow – a man named Jensen – admitted knowing Criff was the man who phoned them, but that's not an improvement on what we had before. How're things?'

Craigie explained, shortly. Trale was silent at the other end of the line for a moment. Then:

'Want me?'

'You'd better come up.'

'Time for me to call at the hospital first?'

'Yes, get here about four,' said Craigie.

He knew that Davidson and Trale were old friends, really close friends, and he could imagine what Trale would feel like if the affair ended fatally for Wally Davidson. Well – it was the game, the same deadly show that would see the end of them all in time – unless, like many of his best agents, they resigned automatically when they married.

The Department had a set rule that no married men should be used, except in an emergency. Craigie was often heartily glad of it, although sometimes he would have given worlds for the services of the older men. But the responsibility of a family and the Department was too much. Craigie had to count on undivided attention.

He picked up the third instrument, hoping it would be word from Lois Dacre. His pencil was poised, but a man's voice came over the wire: moreover an unfamiliar one.

Craigie's body tensed.

'Well, Craigie, isn't it time you drew your men off?'

Very quietly Craigie reached for one of the other telephones.

'That would be rather foolish, wouldn't it, when they're doing so well?'

'Well?' queried the man at the other end of the wire with a macabre laugh. 'Davidson, Carruthers and Falling, all dead or as good as dead. Kerr was lucky but he won't last much longer, and you – but it would be much simpler if you withdrew. After all it doesn't affect you personally, Craigie.'

'Think not?' asked Craigie. 'It seems, however, to effect you that way.'

The voice at the other end sounded less satisfied.

'We warned – '

Craigie laughed, although he was not feeling like laughter. His right finger was tapping out a message: long-short-long-short – he was giving instructions to the man at the other end of the line. It went direct to a secretary who had previously had to take Morse messages in similar emergencies.

The secretary gathered the drift and immediately telephoned the Yard, giving orders for the line connected with Whitehall 12121-8 to be traced immediately.

Craigie stopped tapping at last.

'Aren't you getting a little melodramatic?'

'Possibly,' snapped the other. 'Falling – '

Craigie's eyes narrowed.

'Falling is perhaps the worst angle of this affair that we've touched. But calling me like this is just nonsensical vanity. As bad as Criff's.'

'You think so? You'd be wiser to call it a serious warning. Understand that we're not going to brook interference. We'll act as we have already started, and there won't be a member of your precious Department left unless you withdraw them.'

Craigie was smiling to himself.

'Let me see – I've fifty odd agents in England, and several hundred abroad. This is going to be serious, I can see. You plan a massacre? But just a moment. Why kill Sigmund Prell?'

He knew that he had managed to get a thrust past the speaker, for the voice had grown rasping. But it was an *English* voice. It had a peculiar quality of resonance, not entirely due to the telephone, which made Craigie sure he would be able to recognise it again. And by now the Yard would have been sure to have traced the call.

'We killed Prell because he was likely to get in our way; as we will not hesitate to do to others under the same circumstances. Craigie, I am warning you – '

Craigie's laugh sounded genuinely amused.

'Benevolence, too, it's almost too much. But since warnings are in the air, I'll give you one. You know Criff talked quite a lot before he was unfortunate enough to be shot?'

Again there was a pause, and this time the man at the other end sounded more cautious, as though he was deliberately holding back his temper.

'So – he did?'

'About Prell and other things,' said Graigie. 'A great number of other things. Can I make a counter offer?

'What's that?'

'If you'll come and see me, and talk to me, I'll make it worth your while,' said Craigie. 'I'll guarantee no police action, for instance, against you.'

For some reason or other, the suggestion seemed to worsen his caller's temper. Craigie heard a lurid stream of oaths, then the receiver was banged down. The line had hardly gone dead before there was another ring. Craigie grabbed the receiver.

'Miller here. Craigie, that caller – '

'Where was it from?'

Miller spoke quickly.

'From a call box, Craigie. From the nearest call box to Lane House, Camberley. How does that sound?'

'*Camberley!*' exclaimed Gordon Craigie, and his mind was immediately chasing round on this new angle. The house of Mr Matthew Horn, his brother-in-law Joshua and his nephew Freddie, the house where Doriennet had been murdered, was back in the centre of the stage again.

Chapter 10

Lois Meets A Lady

In common with the other members of the Department Lois Dacre had known that Lady Mondell played a part in this affair. She had also known that her ladyship was suspected of minor espionage, and that Z agents were watching her. Lois knew for instance that young Falling had been detailed to win milady's confidence.

Just prior to seeing Miller outside Devennet Court, Lois had phoned Craigie, telling him something of what had happened. Her appearance there had been solely because she had learned earlier in the morning that Kerr was going to see Criff. Craigie had told her of Falling's death, and with an intuition which helped her where it might have failed a man, Lois had guessed at the real state of affairs between Falling and the ex-actress.

When she had seen Lady Mondell at Devennet Court she had not hesitated to follow her.

For two hours after leaving Miller, she had followed Lady Mondell, and she grew more and more puzzled as the minutes flew.

The other woman seemed to be wandering aimlessly about London. She visited a milliner's, and spent half-an-hour there. She went into a large store, apparently with no real objective, for she walked through three or four floors, and then out again; and all the time Lois had a feeling that she was seeing a woman who was half-insane.

But why?

Lady Mondell could hardly have learned of the Falling murder, or so Lois believed. And, as Craigie had told her, the woman had been to Croydon Airport that morning, had a seat booked on the Paris plane, but for some reason she had not started the journey.

Again, why?

Lois was hoping that she would find out, and wishing that the other woman would settle down. London pavements were not the best places for walking. Only once did Rene take a cab, and that seemed simply to rest for five minutes.

Unless, of course, she was trying to make sure whether or not she was followed.

But there was something in the strained expression of the woman's face that told Lois Dacre that her motive was not caution or cunning. Lady Mondell was wandering aimlessly because she felt aimless, because something was worrying, scaring or frightening her.

At three o'clock, to Lois Dacre's relief, Rene took another cab and ten mintes afterwards she alighted outside the main entrance of Devennet Court.

There were plentiful signs of the fire of the morning. Burned fragments of furniture lay about the pavement and there were deep pools of water in the street.

That part of the building where Rene Mondell had her flat had not been affected. Lois saw her walk towards the lift; she hesitated and then stepped towards one of several telephone kiosks built inside the hall of the court.

She found Craigie's lines engaged, and left a message with Sir William Fellowes at the Yard to the effect that she was at Lady Mondell's flat. Then she walked to the lift, shot upwards and, ten minutes after Lady Mondell's arrival, rang the bell.

Rene herself opened the door.

Lois smiled: she had the kind of smile that could make others take to her at once, and momentarily it seemed to satisfy Rene Mondell.

'I think you had better see me,' said Lois gently.

She had not realised before the extent of the intense misery of the other woman's expression. Few people would have called Rene beautiful just then. Her eyes were shadowed and her lips tightly drawn; she looked ten years more than her age.

'Why?' Even her voice was spiritless.

'Well – it's difficult to say,' said Lois. 'If you will spare me perhaps ten minutes – '

'No, *please*! There's nothing at all I want to buy, and – my maid has left me suddenly, I – ' The woman seemed hysterical.

Lois stepped inside and closed the door behind her. All the time she was warning herself that it might be a trap, that someone else might be in the flat. But she was backing a belief that Rene was alone and that the appearance of misery was genuine.

'Look here,' began Lady Mondell, but Lois Dacre gripped her firmly by the arm and urged her through the hall to the sitting-room. Rene went as though she had not the strength to resist, either mentally or physically.

She sat down, heavily. Lois drew a chair up, and was astonished at the relief to her legs. Then she forgot it, and tried a broadside attack, the approach she had learned from Bob Kerr.

'I've been following you about, Lady Mondell, since you were at the fire this morning. Does that mean anything?'

The words seemed to pierce the coma from which the other woman was suffering and Rene Mondell leaned forward sharply.

'You've been *following* me? But why – '

'Because you were known to be working with Criff,' said Lois. 'I'm working for someone else who is interested.'

'*You* are? But *Craigie* doesn't use women – '

'Who said it was Craigie?' asked Lois gently, but no longer doubtful about this woman's importance; she knew Craigie.

Lois felt that things were working out very well.

She was by no means sure of the outcome of the interview, and there was a possibility that Rene would afterwards talk of her call to others and describe the visitor. It was just as well for the start, at all events, that Rene did not believe she was a Department Z agent. That 'Craigie doesn't use women' had served an excellent purpose in two ways.

Lois smiled.

'England isn't the only country interested in Adam Criff. But before we go into that – '

'I don't know what you want,' said Rene with a sudden fierce intentness, 'but if you're after Criff, he's dead. Thank God! He's made my life a misery and – '

Lois sat back, and waited. She had judged correctly. The woman in front of her was desperately anxious to talk, to rid her mind of a burden: and Lois was a Godsend to her.

The story was vague, but it included talk of work abroad for Criff: of the Paris affair, held so long over her head; of the fact that she had started to *feel* for a man whom she did not name; and that she had learned that Criff had planned to send her to Paris that morning while the unnamed man was being killed.

'How did you learn that?' asked Lois gently. As she had hoped, Rene was hardly conscious of the interruption, although it changed the trend of her thoughts a little.

'It was Shirin. You don't know him, but he phoned me. I – I think Shirin disliked Criff, and Criff was annoyed with him last night. Criff was planning some kind of trick with – with Jim. I came back from the airport at once, and the fire had started. Jim's not at home. I've 'phoned him time and time again, and he's not there. Criff – Criff's dead. But where is Jim?'

Lois Dacre stood up slowly, putting her hand on the other woman's shoulder.

'I'm sorry, Lady Mondell. I can give you some information, but it isn't – pleasant.'

Those dulled eyes widened. A hand clutched at Lois's wrist.

'Jim's not – '

'I'm sorry,' Lois said.

She hated giving the other woman the news, but someone

had to, and perhaps she could do it less brutally than others. Moreover there was a chance that Rene Mondell would be useful to the Department, and Craigie needed everything and everyone now who might help him.

Rene sat very still, and then she burst out:

'If Criff wasn't dead I'd – I'd kill him! The murderer! He must have learned that Jim and me were – '

'He did,' Lois said.

She made up her mind quickly that she could safely say that she was working for Craigie. She believed that Rene Mondell was interested in nothing apart from the death of Falling, and the fact that Criff, and those for whom Criff had worked, had killed him.

'Listen, Lady Mondell. I *am* working for Craigie. I know just what happened. Mr Falling was told, this morning, to come here and see you. You were supposed to be hurt. He suspected a trick, and told – Bob Kerr. You know Kerr?'

'Yes.' Those eyes were almost feverish.

'Well, Falling was kidnapped when he called here. Kerr and two others followed him, but Criff discovered that, and Falling was killed. The man who shot him was killed too – Kerr got him.'

Rene's eyes were incredibly hard.

'The man may have shot him. Criff and – and others really killed him.'

'You're sure?'

'Yes.' Her voice was as hard as her expression.

'If you had an opportunity of working against them, would you take it?'

Rene Mondell pushed her chair back and stood up. Her eyes were much brighter, and her hands were clenched, but her voice was very steady.

'I'd do anything. *Anything*, to – to avenge Jim.'

'I see,' said Lois Dacre quietly. 'Then will you please say nothing to anyone of my visit? Just wait until you hear from me. You've been working for Criff against Craigie. There may be a chance for working for Craigie against those who were behind Criff. I can't promise, but – '

The other woman nodded.

'I understand,' she said. 'I'll be quiet. But it must happen quickly, I can't sit back doing nothing. I – '

She broke off. There was a sharp ring at the front door bell, and both of them stared towards the hall. Rene drew a sharp breath, and then relaxed.

'I wonder who – '

'May I slip into the bedroom?' asked Lois quickly. 'I'll leave the door open, and if it's anyone unpleasant I'll be at hand. It will be as well if I'm not seen.'

Lady Mondell nodded.

'All right. Quickly.'

She seemed to be much stronger now that there was talk of working for Craigie, and Lois felt satisfied. Craigie would at least give the other woman something to do, even if it was unimportant. And they might find a way in which she could be very useful indeed.

The caller, of course, might be anyone. A tradesman, a friend –

Lois left the bedroom door open two inches. She waited by the opening long enough to glimpse the tall, stout man who entered the room. It was no one she had seen before, and she felt a little disappointed. She heard his voice, deep, cultured, persuasive. 'I promise you, Lady Mondell, I shall not waste your time,' he was saying, as Rene closed the front door. Without being invited the big man sat in an easy chair. He looked about him, as though commenting mentally on the luxury of the apartment.

'What is it you want?'

The visitor turned a pair of smallish eyes towards Rene Mondell.

'I have come, Lady Mondell, with an important message. Are you alone?'

'I don't know that I like your question,' said Rene sharply. 'What is it you want? I can of course telephone for assistance if I need it.'

'My dear lady!' The big man laughed lightly. 'My visit is strictly proper, I promise you. Strictly proper! You know, of course, of the sad death of Mr Criff?'

Rene's voice was expressionless.

'I do.'

'And you worked for him, just as I did,' said the big man. 'Believe me, he was a foolish fellow. He was much too big for his boots, much too big. It was decided some days ago that he would have to die. I was informed of this, although I believe other members of our little fraternity were left in ignorance. But now there is still work to do.'

It seemed incredible to Lois that Rene Mondell could remain so unmoved. She would not have done but for her first caller: that was reasonably certain. Now she was playing a part, a part suggested by Lois, and she was playing it well.

'I see. Who sent you, Mr – '

'My name is Smith, dear lady.' The man's wide grin told Rene that he was lying. 'My principals – and *your* principals, suggested the call. Your beauty, my dear Lady Mondell, and your ability, will make you invaluable. I am requested to offer you two thousand pounds a year, as a retaining fee, and one hundred pounds for each week you are actively working for the fraternity, if you will continue with us. You can be assured that your work will be under much more astute direction than it was with Adam Criff.

There was a moment's silence, and Lois wondered whether the man would see that Rene was acting: and she wondered also whether the older woman would crack under this strain.

Rene did not, for her voice was steady enough if a little more tense.

'I – don't know. I'm not interested in money, Mr Smith, and I'm tired of the whole business. Tired to death of it!'

Mr Smith raised his brows, and shifted his hands from his paunch to the arms of his chair.

'I see, I see. A pity, Lady Mondell. But I feel that you will be well advised to accept a most generous offer. Adam Criff remembered to report a little affair in Paris, only a year or so ago. Most sad – and most unfortunate if your part – '

There was venom in Rene Mondell's voice, but her acting now was really superb. The shock of learning that Falling had died seemed to have given her a sharper intelligence.

'I see. Blackmail. Well – supposing I refuse? I didn't kill that man in Paris – '

Mr Smith turned his methods.

'I do not doubt it, my dear Lady Mondell. But you will admit that circumstances seemed to be against you. But please, please do not think of blackmail. After all, our offer is very generous indeed.'

Rene walked to the side of the room, took a cigarette from a box and lit it thoughtfully.

'I see. I'll think it over, Mr Smith.'

'I would much rather have your decision now, please.'

'I can't make up my mind immediately, please understand that,' she said decisively. 'Say some time tomorrow morning, if you will call again.'

'Very good, very good.' Mr Smith seemed reasonably satisfied, and heaved himself from his chair. 'I shall call, say, at ten o'clock?'

'I probably won't be up until eleven.'

Mr. Smith chuckled.

'Very understandable in so beautiful a woman. Then half-past eleven, Lady Mondell. Be sure please to have your answer, and be earnestly advised by me to accept the suggestion. *Good* afternoon.'

Rene showed him to the door. Lois could hear his footsteps – surprisingly light ones for so heavy a man – as he hurried along the passage.

Lois moved from the bedroom, and taking the other's arm, stepped to the window.

On the opposite side of the road was a Morris saloon, with a youngish-looking man at the wheel. A few second later the flabby Mr Smith appeared and climbed into a two-seater of ancient vintage. The cars moved off in quick succession, and no matter how suspicious Mr Smith might be of the driver of the Morris, he would have to admit that the other car started slightly ahead of him.

Rene Mondell was frowning.

'What does that mean?'

'It means that Smith will be followed,' said Lois. 'Well – do you see now how you *might* be able to help?'

The other nodded. The weariness of her expression had gone. She looked stronger than she had before; she *was* stronger.

'You mean I can work for Criff's people, *and* for Craigie?'

'Do you think you can?'

Rene Mondell laughed. It was not a humorous sound and it was not pleasant; her eyes seemed to be looking past Lois. She was seeing the light-haired, smiling and cheerful youngster who had made her fall in love, and she was picturing, too, what he looked like dead.

'I'm sure I can. They killed Jim – '

And then, the storm came. Lois knew she could do nothing to stop or ease it. Rene Mondell simply collapsed into a chair and cried, cried as Lois had never seen a woman cry before.

Lois, with her practical mind, slipped into the kitchenette and made coffee. When she returned the paroxysm was over, and Rene Mondell, bright-eyed and steady-lipped, looked towards her.

'I'm sorry. Now tell me what I must do.'

* * *

While Dodo Trale was following the flabby Mr Smith, while Lois and Rene were drinking coffee, while a pug-faced man was talking on the telephone to Mr Kryn, and while three agents of Craigie's were on their way to Camberley in the hope of finding a man with a deep, resonant voice, Craigie, Sir William Fellowes and Superintendent Miller were gathered in Craigie's office. They had discussed the affair at some length, and there seemed nothing more they could discuss, when the telephone, which had interrupted them half-a-dozen times, rang again.

Craigie left his armchair and lifted the receiver. Miles Bettin's voice came over the wires, sharp and precise as always.

'Craigie?'

'Yes, carry on, Bettin.'

'There's more news from Vallena,' said Bettin sharply. 'They've done two things. Openly accused the Soviet of arranging Prell's murder – '

'We expected that.'

'It's going to make things stickier in mid-Europe,' complained Bettin. 'But that's not all, and the other things affect us more directly. They've doubled the tariff on *all* British goods, and fixed a minimum of fifty per cent. The thin edge of the wedge, eh?'

Craigie's lips pursed.

'Yes, and not so thin, perhaps. But what's the connection between Prell's assassination and the tariff? That's our problem.'

'You'd better send the best man you've got over there,' said Bettin. 'I – '

Bettin stopped, with an exclamation. He shouted, "Craigie!" and then there came, very clearly to Craigie's ears, the sharp crack of a pistol shot. The telephone at the other end clattered downwards with a rattling din, and then Craigie heard a whispered message.

"They've got me. A very tall – thin – man.'

And then the voice stopped.

Chapter 11

Freddie Sings Again

The murder of Miles Bettin was one of those tragedies that it was impossible to hush up. But there were some things that could be done to lessen publicity. An urgent meeting of the Cabinet was called within half-an-hour of the shooting. Apparently no one in the Foreign Office had noticed anything amiss. Fellowes and Miller were not unknown in Bettin's office, and with the help of one or two discreet under-secretaries, the leakage of information would not reach the Press prior to the meeting, unless the tall, lean man named Kryn had told the papers.

The Rt Hon. David Wishart, the then Premier, distinguished, a little inclined to dally, but popular and honest, could always be relied on in an emergency. And as often happened he had arranged for Craigie to be present at 10, Downing Street.

Wishart told the others about the trouble, and had to wait five minutes before the sensation died down. Craigie gave a first-hand recital of what he had heard, and waited for the outburst of questions. Did he know who? Did he know why?

'It's directly connected with Vallena,' said Craigie.

He could see the disbelief on the faces of those august gentlemen who led the Government. None of them was likely to take Vallena seriously. Why, it was no more than the size of Wales, a small, hilly, agricultural country, with no statesmen worth thinking of, and an irresponsible playgirl Princess with a Prince whose morals belonged to the farmyard.

The voice of Jonathan Scott rose above the rest.

'Look here, Craigie, let us get this quite straight. Are you seriously suggesting that Prell and Bettin have been murdered, and there's a chance of other foreign secretaries going the same way?'

Craigie forced a smile.

'There is no doubt that Prell was murdered, and by the same people – '

The crotchety Secretary for War muttered a very audible 'Nonsense!'

'I don't think so, sir.'

'Couldn't get from Baj to London in the time, Craigie. Be sensible, man, be sensible!'

'I said "people",' Craigie said drily. 'There's an association working in England and Vallena, and the two murders were unquestionably connected. Bettin described the murderer to me before he died. He is the same man who shot, or ordered the shooting, of Adam Criff.'

He kept his temper with difficulty. There were times when he detested the English habit of assuming that anything abnormal just could not happen. When he was thinking yards ahead of the others it was an irritating trait to argue against.

'Criff, eh? Criff, Bettin and Prell!' This from the Secretary for War.

Craigie looked across at Sir Michael Lane, the then Secretary of the Board of Trade, and minister without portfolio.

'Can you tell us anything of trade relationship with Vallena, Sir Michael?'

He hoped Lane would prove convincing. Lane was. He had, he said, been disturbed by the news of an emergency meeting at a time when he had just learned of the prohibitive tariff put on British goods entering Vallena. Something would have to be done to stop the hostile attitude of that country, but, knowing the trouble there had been of late with shipments, he had no idea how it could be done.

'And there,' Craigie resumed as Lane finished, 'you have

as much as I know, gentlemen. Criff has not been operating only for himself, but for others. One of the others was Sigmund Prell. Prell, Criff and others so far unknown, are bent on breaking Vallenian trade with England – '

'Won't make much difference, will it?' demanded the Home Secretary. He was a man whose intellectual ability hardly attained the level expected of one in his position. He was, however, both hard-working and conscientious, and a little overwhelmed by the fact that a persuasive tongue and an ability to sway multitudes of voters at election time had given him such an exalted rank.

Michael Lane snorted: 'Not much difference! At least a hundred and fifty millions a year goes through Vallena, Harris!'

Harris pulled a thick underlip a little nervously.

'Does it, then. Didn't realise it.'

Wishart said quickly: 'What are you doing, Craigie?'

'As much as I can. Bettin mentioned a man who had already been connected with this business, but I can't tell you a great deal about him yet. A Matthew Horn, head of and export firm, and living near Camberley.'

He had half-hoped that one of the others present would be able to say a word about Horn, but the name obviously meant nothing to them.

'Well – it isn't a thing we can handle secretly. And the connection with Prell will be assumed, if nothing worse. I'm afraid we shall have some trouble.' Wishart felt, and looked, tired out.

Craigie spoke quickly.

'We could say that the murderer is known, Wishart. It's true, up to a point – I know the man but can't put my fingers on him.'

'How will that help?' asked Jonathan Scott practically.

'We'll be able to say it was for private reasons,' Craigie answered. 'A personal quarrel. If we give that story out to the Press as semi-official, they will make a great deal more of it than the somewhat nebulous connection with Prell. It won't cause half as much alarm, and it will give us time to work.'

As he had expected there was considerable argument. But Wishart, Scott, Lane and Harris were all with him, and the decision to do as he said was carried by a fifty per cent majority. Craigie waited just long enough to make sure of it, and then left the Cabinet to it.

Miller and Fellowes themselves had gone down to Camberley. Craigie proposed to follow. He was missing Kerr a lot more than he had expected. It had become a habit to rely on the ex-flying ace.

He called at his office to make sure that no messages were waiting, and then started for Camberley in his own car, an Armstrong Siddeley that had rendered him good service. In front and behind him were police cars, and on the same road were cars with his agents at the wheels. Craigie had stopped being careless, but for the life of him he could not understand why Bettin had been murdered.

He thought back.

The very tall man had been seen in the corridors of the Foreign Office, but it was not unusual to see unknown faces there. No one had seen him leave the building.

Every policeman in England was on the look-out for Mr Kryn. It was a search as widespread as Craigie and the Yard had ever instituted. Airfields, shipping ports, termini and main roads were all watched with lynx-eyed care for a man standing six foot and a half; but Craigie had a premonition that he would not be found.

* * *

Mr Freddie Kingham had been despondent ever since Doriennet's death.

It had been a horrible shock to him, though he had derived some satisfaction from being able to send that secret message to Miss Dale – as he knew Lois Dacre. Her thanks had been warm, and Freddie had hoped to see her again. Alone.

Instead a tough-looking cove named Kerr had arrived, with others. They had brought Lois Dale, it was true, but she had hardly seemed to notice him. Moreover, they had brought a man who had been wounded in both legs, and commandeered his, Freddie's bedroom while the doctor did his job. The result had been a horrible smell of antiseptic which had ruined his night's sleep. In fact he had slept worse that first night than any time he could remember, even in the days when he had been frowned on – together with his father and brother – by Uncle Matt.

He could not forget Doriennet's battered head. Ugh! A grisly business altogether, and he hoped to goodness they wouldn't want him at the inquest.

Gloomily Freddie had dressed. As gloomily he had staggered through a late breakfast. Bennet had served it, looking like a ghost. His father, who had been out late on the previous night, sent a message down that he was unwell. Uncle Matthew, for once, had breakfasted in bed. Beastly. Ugh!

There had been a light relief for the next day. Uncle Matt had decided that until the inquest was over – yes, Freddie *would* be wanted – it was better not to go into the office. That was a little cheering, but the whole position was pretty nasty. He did think of getting the Singer out, for it was a glorious day, but he jibbed at going into the garage.

The inquest was for Tuesday. Pretty decent of Uncle Matt to give him two days off. No 'nose to the grindstone' fuss about Uncle Matt. A great fellow.

The only member of the household who seemed unaffected by the murder had been Martha, the cook, a cheerful, garrulous soul, easily persuaded on the day of the inquest to cook his favourite dish.

Freddie ate, and grew more cheerful. He took the car out of the garage with little or no qualms, had a fast spin, and came back to find three cars parked outside Lane House, and a remarkable number of lean and tough-looking men in and around the grounds.

Browning, dressed in the same dilapidated grey suit, looked mutinously up at his young employer as Freddie entered the garage.

'What's all the crowd about, Browning?'

The shell-shocked handyman muttered something that he obviously believed Freddie was too young to understand, and then:

'Can't move a n'inch wivvout 'em, Master Fred. Bloomin' nuisance they are – bloomin' busies.'

For the first time that day Freddie really laughed.

'You don't seem to like 'em, Browning. Their job, after all, and they can't help it.'

'What I want to know is, why don't they look for the feller that did it, instead've comin' here?'

'Ask me,' said Freddie.

He parked the car and moved off, humming cheerfully under his breath and looking for anything which might suggest that Miss Dale was here. No luck. Nor, for that matter, did he recognise the man Kerr or his companions. A fresh bunch had come down.

Uncle Matt would probably be sore about it.

Freddie went up to his room, considerably lighter in mood. After all, he had not known the dead man at all, and it was hard to be sorry about a fellow you only knew by the letter-heading of his business paper.

'Mr. Kingham, sir.'

It was Bennet, a Bennet who looked scared out of his life. He was standing in the doorway leading to the bathroom, white-lipped and trembling.

'Good Lord! What's the trouble, Bennet?'

'Your – your uncle, sir. I think the – the police are going to – to take him, sir.'

Freddie stood still, staring aghast at the butler. His stupefaction seemed to split him asunder. Uncle Matt going with the police? Good God almighty it was impossible!

'He's – *what*?'

'The – the police, sir – '

'Oh, but look here, he's one of the best,' said Freddie loudly. 'It's all nonsense. I'd better go and see them – '

He had no idea what he would say if he did see them, but had a desperate urge to do and say something. Hang it, even the police had sense, and to arrest a man like Uncle Matthew was crazy. Haywire. Freddie started manfully for the door.

'Sir!' Bennet's voice was pitiable.

'All right, Bennet, I won't do anything rash.'

'It isn't that, sir. It's – Mr Matthew asked me to – to give you these papers, sir. Whatever happens you are to keep them, sir. There – there's a letter from him as well.'

Bennet, speaking in a whisper that only just reached the younger man's ears, was holding out two envelopes. Freddie turned resolutely from the door.

'When did he give you these?'

'He – he told me you were to have them if the police came sir. You were to hide them – the letter – '

Bennet was obviously incapable of coherent thought. Poor blighter, he had worked for Matthew for fifteen years, Freddie reminded himself. Damned blow, to find the man you work for wanted by the police on a murder charge. But it was absurd, no man in his right senses would suspect Uncle Matthew of any crime. As for the murder of that cove Doriennet, why, Uncle Matt had been in the house all the time.

Freddie forgot that he was not sure how long Doriennet had been dead. He scowled as he took the papers.

'You – you aren't to say a word, sir, to anyone.'

'Right-ho, Bennet, don't you worry. But hang it, there's no reason why I shouldn't go along and see those idiots!'

'I – I should read the letter first, sir.'

Freddie hesitated, and then ripped open the smaller envelope. The other was heavily sealed, and the only writing on it was in the top left hand corner, where three letters had been written, with three figures following:

UMY – 854

'Odd,' decided Freddie.

He did not see the cunning gleam in Bennet's eyes as the butler slipped out of the room. He turned the paper from the small envelope over twice, and scowled. For there was no letter. Only a few words were written on the paper, and Uncle Matt's easily recognisable initials were scrawled beneath.

Keep these until called for by someone quoting UMY – 854. Ask no questions. M.H.

'Well – I'm – damned!' decided Freddie.

He stared down at the sealed envelope, and then wondered what the devil would happen if the police found them in his possession. Well, he had the letter to show that he had not kept them for long. It was not dated though, unusual for Uncle Matthew, who usually dated everything, from a pay envelope to a memo about the wastage of pencil leads in the general office.

Freddie almost fell a victim to a ravenous curiosity. Above all things he wanted to know what was in the envelope, what the mysterious papers contained. Did they hold the solution of the murder?

If they did, should he not go to the police?

That loyalty which Lois Dacre had read in Freddie Kingham's face showed itself again. Damn it, he was half-assuming that Uncle Matt did know something about Doriennet's murder, and that was silly.

He had never before realised just how unpleasant and yet intriguing it was to hide something from the police. There was a spice of danger and adventure in it. Adventure! He – but where should he put it? If the police took Uncle Matt, he reasoned, they would search the house pretty thoroughly. No use putting stuff like that in the lining of his suit, for instance, Oh, Lord, and he had not been to see Uncle Matt yet.

Freddie considered a hiding place thoughtfully.

He dismissed several possibilities as too obvious. It was surprisingly difficult to find a place where you could hide an envelope of any size. And he could not put it anywhere in the grounds, because of that crowd of police, or whoever they were.

Freddie Kingham suddenly remembered the grim-faced man Kerr. If Kerr should come after him –

'Blast it!' snapped Freddie aloud. 'I'll keep it in my pocket, they probably won't search me. I'll make 'em get a warrant before they do, anyhow.'

Annoyed, pugnacious, a little scared and vastly intrigued, Kingham tucked both envelopes in his pocket and hurried out of the room. He saw two plain-clothes men, actually Department Z agents, in the hall. They seemed to be guarding the drawing-room door. Freddie walked towards them.

'Sorry, son. Thc room is engaged for a few minutes.'

The speaker was a tall, cumbersome-looking man named Loftus, one of Craigie's brightest young agents.

Freddie frowned. The 'son' went right under his skin.

'It's my house,' he said mildly.

'Well – Mr Horn's, shall we say?'

That was the last straw. Freddie glared at the man, pushed past him, and had the handle of the door turning before Loftus could stop him. Loftus grabbed the youngster's arm, and Freddie, who had one big art – that of self-defence – sent a surprisingly fast short-arm jab towards Loftus's middle.

But Loftus was not there to take it.

He dodged and, being large, simply lifted Freddie off his feet. Kingham struggled, and as he did so the envelope, with the lettering 'UMY – 854', dropped with a loud plop on to the floor.

Chapter 12

Bad for Matthew Horn

Five hours sleep, a moderately satisfying meal, treatment of minor burns, and cold compresses on a twisted ankle, did a great deal to make Bob Kerr feel capable of working.

He asked for his clothes so that he could get up. The nurse and the doctor refused. He was not well enough to get up: it would in fact be madness for him to get up, and if he put any weight on the injured ankle he would be in bed for a week.

Without a trace of that delirium that had worried Craigie, Kerr eased himself up in bed and regarded both nurse and doctor.

'I'm getting up,' he said. 'If my clothes aren't here within three minutes, I'll get up without them. You're probably quite right and I'm probably a ruddy fool, but I'm getting up.'

The doctor wanted to swear at him. Sir Wilfred Mayer had gone off duty, and the other had no idea who Kerr was. He had been told he was the famous flying ace, but fame outside medical research meant nothing to that earnest physician.

'Now, Mr Kerr – '

Kerr flung the bedclothes off, and climbed out of bed, careful to stand only on his left foot. He grabbed a small chair, and using it as a walking stick he started for the door.

The doctor shrugged helplessly.

'All right. As we're short of strait-jackets you may have your clothes. But I take no responsibility.'

Kerr smiled disarmingly.

'I really do appreciate your efforts. I'm all wrong, I know, but I can get about at a pinch, and I've a desperately urgent reason for wanting to be off right now. By the way, my friends in the other ward – Davidson and Carruthers.'

The doctor unbent a little, and the nurse slipped out for Kerr's clothes and a crutch. What an astonishing change in the man when he smiled!

'Mr Davidson will be all right, there's no question of it. Three or four days here, and then a week or two's rest. Mr Carruthers – well, there's every chance, but he's not out of danger yet. The throat wound went very deep. I wonder' – the doctor looked at Kerr curiously – 'how it happened. Not suicide, surely?'

Kerr laughed.

'Certainly not suicide, doctor. Murder attempted but murder not done, thank heavens. Ah, nurse, you're a friend in a thousand.'

She helped him dress, and he hobbled out of the ward with the help of a crutch. He felt damned silly, but he supposed it was wise to use the thing. He spent five minutes in Wally Davidson's ward, thankful to find Davidson able to speak and smile.

'What happened at Criff's, Wally?'

'That blasted little runt of a servant,' said Davidson with a scowl. 'I've told Trale. Carry and I took the beggar for granted, I'm afraid, and he pulled a gun on us. A couple of minutes later that Kryn fellow came in, and a brace of others. We were hit over the head so effectively that we neither saw nor felt what happened next.'

Kerr looked grim.

'You know they got Criff?'

'Yes. How're things?'

'With the aid of my crutch I'm going to find out,' said Kerr with a grin. 'Keep it up, old man.'

Davidson gave the ghost of a grin as Kerr hobbled out. A porter fetched him a taxi, and at eight o'clock, when darkness had just settled over London, Kerr reached Craigie's office.

Craigie was in.

* * *

'And so it looks bad for Matthew Horn,' said Gordon Craigie some half-an-hour afterwards. 'I don't think there's any doubt that he had the papers, and they prove his complicity with Criff up to the hilt.'

'Hmn,' said Kerr. 'Horn says he didn't give them to the butler, doesn't he?'

'Yes. But Bennet seems genuine, he's worked for Horn for fifteen years. Young Kingham admits that the initials are in his uncle's writing, and he's obviously dying to say they're not. And remember Bettin mentioned Horn.'

'I suppose Bettin had learned something and was holding out on you,' grunted Kerr.

'Looks like it, poor fellow. And of course Kryn knew he knew, and aimed to stop him passing the news on. It's a bad show altogether.'

'Where's Horn now?'

'We brought him up to Cannon Street.'

'Did he know of Bettin's murder beforehand?'

'Well – he said not. But he came precious near to giving himself away. I taxed him with it, and – well, it was just an impression. I think he either knew or expected it.'

'And yet he won't say a word?'

'He says plenty. Chiefly that he did not give the papers to Bennet, that he does not know what 'UMY – 854' means, that he has never had any business with Adam Criff, private or otherwise.'

Kerr lit a cigarette, and propped his foot a little higher on a stool in front of him.

'And "UMY – 854" is the number that Stefan Vonovitch, who murdered Prell, is registered with at the Soviet Secret Service. The papers comprise a list of Criff's activities in organising the gang at Grattle Street, an outline of the arrangements to kill Doriennet, your humble servant, and others. All past events, Gordon. If I'd been Horn I'd have burned the damned things.'

'There were suggestions for further work,' said Craigie, 'but they don't mean much. They foreshadow the blockade against English goods, too. But there's no apparent reason why Horn should have kept them, and sent them with the message to young Kingham.'

Kerr shook his head.

'I don't like it, Gordon, it looks like a frame-up. Supposing someone else gave them to Bennet, with the instructions to pass them on as he did? It saves the other fellow, and it covers everything by putting Horn on the spot. Who else have we got to consider down there, now?'

'Young Kingham, and his father.'

'An ineffective but pleasant youngster, and a feckless artist, both dependent on Matthew Horn for a livelihood. Then there's Bennet, and the other servants, while I met a queer customer named Browning the other day. Did you see him?'

'Queer's the word,' said Craigie. 'But harmless. Shell-shock.'

'People have called me harmless,' Kerr said with a grin. 'I see that the Press have labelled Bettin's murder as the end of a private feud. A good idea, but I'll bet it wasn't Wishart's.'

'It wasn't,' said Craigie, drily. 'Now, Bob. It's reasonable to assume that Bettin had been in touch with Matthew Horn, *or* had reason to believe Horn was in the affair. And to stop him from talking, he was killed. Prell was killed in Baj in exactly the same way and for the same reason. Now Bettin either had the wrong end of the stick, or Horn *does* know something.'

'I'd like to see him,' said Kerr. 'Can we have him here? By the way, have you heard from Lois lately?'

Craigie telephoned for Matthew Horn to be brought over – Superintendent Miller was still on duty and would look after it in person – and then answered the second question.

'Lois is doing very well, Bob. She discovered that Mondell was working for Criff, and that she fell in love with young Falling, as he did with her. Now that he's dead, Mondell is prepared to do anything to avenge him. Her own words. We shall probably find her very useful, as she's been asked to carry on with the other side.'

Kerr's eyes gleamed.

'And is she going to?'

'She says she will. I daren't give her too much information, of course, in case she talks under pressure, but when you get over to Baj it will be useful to have her there.'

Kerr grimaced.

'At this rate I'll be in Baj in a month's time, when the shindy's over. Joking apart, it will be three days before I can stand on both feet decently.'

Craigie shrugged his shoulders.

'It can't be helped. I want you to go, and I've a feeling that things will quieten down for a bit. Well now – how does it strike you, as far as we've gone?'

Kerr said it struck him as being the most unholy mess ever, with odds and ends everywhere. But when he and Craigie had worked it out, they realised the odds and ends were not so many, and the answers to a few pertinent questions would cover all the other irrelevancies.

Things like Doriennet's murder, Falling's death, the chasing about London, the fire at Devennet Court, Bettin's assassination together with Prell's, were all smaller factors in the major questions. And the major questions were:

1. For whom had Criff been working?
2. How many of the members of the organisation still remained in England?
3. Why were trade relations being broken between England and Vallena, and if the answer was the obvious one – for individuals to profit by the trade that

would be taken by someone else – who was most likely to benefit?

4. Was Horn telling the truth?
5. Were there any reasons for suspecting that the original political possibilities of civil war in Vallena still existed?
6. If so, what effect would the cessation of English trade have on such a war?
7. Apart from (a) civil war possibilities and (b) individual profit-making by persons unknown, was anything happening that *might* be calculated to make England alter her attitude towards the mid-European situation?
8. (And to Craigie the most important). Was some other power behind the Vallenian organisation, and had that power any ill-intent towards England?

'And if it isn't political, covering items 5, 6, 7 and 8,' said Bob Kerr, 'why did they fear that we would butt in? They must have known that what they were doing would attract our attention or they would not have gone bald-headed for us.'

'That's exactly what we said after you'd seen Doriennet,' said Craigie rather wearily. 'And – here's someone.'

The little green light in the mantelpiece showed, and a few seconds later Miller came in with Matthew Horn.

Despite a harassing time – bordering, he claimed, on third degree – Horn still spoke with that surprisingly unflurried voice. He steadfastly denied having given Bennet the papers. On the other hand he said that Bennet had given him fifteen years of first-class service.

Kerr asked a few questions, some trivial and some important, but could not shake the story. Horn was taken away, apparently convinced that he was the victim of a frame-up.

'And I wouldn't be surprised if he's telling the truth,' said Kerr. 'You're having Bennet and young Kingham watched? And the father?'

'Yes. Freddie Kingham's worked up about the whole

affair,' said Craigie with a slow smile. 'His father's a different sort. A pontifical old devil, and his chief concern seems to be what will happen to him if his brother is convicted of murder.'

'Does Horn keep him altogether?'

'Practically. Kingham sells a few pictures occasionally, but it amounts to no more than beer money. He's well known in practically every Camberley pub.'

'Hm,' said Kerr, 'Horn seems a generous type of fellow.'

Craigie shrugged.

'He's done well, his in-laws haven't. A man with a family conscience complex. All his staff have been with him for years. A cook told me that he was extremely fond of his sister, Kingham's wife, and kept the family because of her. There was a quarrel three years ago, but apparently it was patched up.'

'Who's she favour?' demanded Kerr.

'She's devoted to Horn – all the servants are – and she likes Freddie. She's no time for Joshua Kingham, whom she calls a sponging wastrel. She also says that the other Kingham brother, Samuel, is as bad as his father. He has a bad reputation with women.'

Kerr's slanting brows raised.

'Hm. And that caused the one quarrel.'

'Apparently. Samuel was upsetting the maids, and he acted badly by one or two of them. On the understanding that he went to the colonies, Matthew Horn continued his allowance, and also looked after the other two. Samuel Kingham's in Africa, and they hear from him once a month, when he acknowledges his allowance. On the surface of it, they're the last family in the world to be mixed up in a show like this, but I can't see how we can let them out altogether. Horn *must* know something or Bettin would not have mentioned him.'

'Unless,' said Kerr, harping back on the old line, 'Bettin had wrong information. Oh well, I'll get back. If I nurse the ankle for a day, and start for Baj, say, on Wednesday morning, it should be usable by the time I get there.'

Craigie nodded, and half-smiled.

'Think Lois would like a trip?'

'I took it for granted,' Kerr said with a cheerful grin.

But making his way laboriously to 77g, Brook Street, Kerr was filled with a nagging anxiety.

If they weren't damned careful, there would be a flare-up of some kind, involving England deeply and dangerously. It did not look like a war stunt: but if it robbed England of several hundred millions of trade per annum, it was big enough to justify the trouble that had already been stirred.

With luck, he would learn more about it in Baj, Vallena.

* * *

About the time that Kerr left Craigie's office, a monoplane dropped down on to a private airfield on the outskirts of Baj.

One of the four passengers, a very tall man, would have been recognised by anyone in Craigie's Department, or by the police. Mr Kryn was home again.

With Kryn was a young, pug-faced man, sometimes called Brown but more often known by the name of Herrod. Herrod was not too pleased with life: Kryn had not been entirely deceived by that story of Craigie's lucky escape from a bullet in the back.

The third passenger was von Hauf, the fourth, Gregaroff Shirin.

The four men hurried to a waiting Rolls Royce and were taken as luxuriously as possible – for Vallena was an exceedingly hilly country, and the roads were bad – towards the centre of the city.

At a large house not far from the royal palace, occupied by the reigning Prince Renol, the Rolls Royce stopped.

They were admitted by a liveried footman. Shirin, von Hauf and Herrod were ushered into one of the palatial reception rooms, while Kryn went, unattended, up the stairs.

He reached a door painted black, and pressed a bell-push

sharply, three or four times. There was a pause, and a click. Kryn opened the door, and entered the most depressing room, perhaps that he had ever been in.

It was windowless, the ceiling of painted glass, the floor carpeted a dull black. The luxurious furniture carried still further this sombre hue.

The room had only one occupant – a woman.

She sat at a black desk in a black chair, and she was dressed entirely in black. Not a shade of relief showed, apart from the dead whiteness of her face, and her hands, until one saw her hair. It was of Titian red, coiled about her head in a superb coiffure.

'Well, Kryn?'

She spoke in English, her voice, rather pleasant and musical, completely free from the melodrama that might have been expected from such bizarre surroundings.

Kryn bowed.

'I had your orders, Highness, and I have returned.'

'The others are with you?'

'Those you told to come.'

'That is well, Kryn. You had a good journey?'

'Excellent, Highness.'

'And the situation in England?'

'I think it can safely be said that no one suspects the truth, Highness.'

For the first time her face relaxed.

'That is good, Kryn. You left evidence behind you pointing to the fact that you have come to Vallena?'

'Your orders have been obeyed in every detail, Highness.'

She nodded again.

'We are nearly ready, then. The woman Mondell – she is coming?'

'She has not yet said so, Highness, but it is almost certain. We shall be advised by eleven-thirty, English time, tomorrow.'

'And her husband?'

'He will be cared for.'

'I see. And now – Kerr. He is still alive. He has so many lives that man. I am almost convinced that he is as dangerous as I have been told.'

'He is a man,' said Kryn simply.

'And mortal.' She laughed.

'Now that they will know where you are, Kerr will come. His injury is not serious?'

'I do not think it will detain him more than two or three days, Highness.'

'Will he bring others?'

'It is likely.'

'I should like to see Kerr,' she said slowly, 'before he dies. He sounds interesting. Well, Kryn, progress has been well-maintained here, you see. The tariff has gone through, much against the Prince's wishes, but it has gone through. The first of many. And we are already estranged from Moscow. It was foolish of Moscow to allow Vonovitch to assassinate the unfortunate Sigmund, eh, Kryn?'

For once the man's dark eyes showed a lurking smile.

'Most unfortunate, your Highness. Russia, and soon England, will be offended. And then – '

'And then,' said Katrina, Princess of Vallena, 'we shall see, eh, Kryn, what those great countries can make of our tiny state? All right, Kryn, you may rest.'

Chapter 13

Lull

The lull that Craigie and Kerr had sensed, came, and Craigie, not knowing how carefully it had been arranged, had an opportunity for thinking even harder round the situation, and for tying up several odds and ends.

Helped in no small measure by the insistence of Lois Dacre, Kerr managed to spend a full twenty-four hours on a couch, with his foot up. The swelling was down considerably by the evening, and the doctor who had been summoned and ordered to get it right within thirty-six hours considered the thing possible: what he had not thought possible was to get Kerr resting for that stretch of time.

After six o'clock Lois was finished for the day. She packed a suitcase for the coming trip to Baj, and then went on to Kerr's flat.

'Rene Mondell has had orders to go to Baj,' she told him.

'Good heavens! That needs thinking about. Anything else?'

'Nothing worth reporting. Horn still sticks to his story, and so does Bennet. One of them is lying. Young Freddie Kingham was at the Yard today, trying to tell them it was absurd to keep his uncle. I rather like young Freddie.'

'Anything of his sire?'

'No, nothing from him. Should there be?'

Kerr looked thoughtful.

'Well, someone in or around that place knows something. Bennet might be an accessory, but I can't picture him in a leading part. That leaves young Kingham and his father, if Horn's not guilty.'

'Aren't you rather holding a brief for Horn?'

Kerr laughed ruefully.

'Perhaps I am. He seems a good type, and his record is excellent. There's no breath of scandal in the trade against him. I was on the phone to Craigie this afternoon, and he says that every word is a good one for Matthew Horn.'

'Yet all he's done is to deny everything.'

Kerr looked up at her with a gleam in his eyes.

'*All*, sweetheart?'

'He could have – well – '

Kerr leaned forward and ruffled her hair.

'I know. He could have pitched some story about guessing what was coming to Bettin, about a dozen and one things. Instead he pleads absolute ignorance of the whole affair.'

'And someone at Lane House was in it.'

'We're going round in circles,' said Kerr, 'we said that two or three minutes ago. Perhaps Joshua's the man, but I doubt it. More likely I'm holding a losing brief, and Matthew Horn is a darker horse than I've been able to see. Light me a cigarette, will you, I feel lazy. I – oh, damn!'

It was Mold, at the door, and behind him Dodo Trale, smiling and lifting a hand in salute.

'Sorry to disturb you, but blame Craigie. He tells me I've got to take you both to Baj. It was a blow, but I stood up to it manfully. Listen, Bob, be reasonable, I haven't had a drink since ever.'

Mold was getting used to the ways of these hearty and thirsty friends of his employer. He arrived with beer and a tankard. Dodo Trale twinkled at Lois.

'Disapprove?'

'You fellows pass my comprehension,' Lois admitted.

'Only to be expected,' agreed Trale, 'as we frequently pass our own.' He drank deeply. 'Loftus is going over tomorrow, with young Oundle. That'll be the four of us, and the baggage. Craigie's keeping in touch with Baj, of course, but nothing seems to be reported out of the ordinary.'

'Only a murder of a Foreign Secretary and the strangulation of our trade,' said Kerr. He looked round sharply.

'What the devil's that?'

Dodo lifted his tankard and paused. From outside there came the unmistakable sound of a man, singing. It grew nearer, and the door opened.

Mr William Loftus stood on the threshold.

He was a tall man and wide, and had but one disadvantage as far as Craigie was concerned: he was easily recognisable.

He announced solemnly that he was going to Baj with them and had decided to do so as a stocking vender.

Lois grinned.

'Have you told Craigie yet?'

'No.'

'Oh, my God!' moaned Kerr. 'And I have to try and use you fellows. Listen, thick-head, trade relations with Vallena are at a standstill. Heard about that? Standstill. An Englishman can't sell goods there. A German could. Can you speak German?'

'Like a native,' said Loftus, who was not by nature modest. 'Spent four years there.'

Kerr was moving to the telephone. In ten minutes he had arranged with Craigie that Loftus could have his hair clipped very close, should be found a suit that did not fit him of German cut, and should travel as a representative of a certain Rhine wine establishment.

Loftus accepted it all meekly. He was, he said, always willing to learn. In the next few hours Craigie was in touch with his Berlin agent, the real name and address of a genuine Cologne firm was taken, and in the London–Budapest plane next morning – which went via Berlin – William Loftus travelled as Herr Gustav Schmidt, together with a passport and photograph, ostensibly German.

One or two other things had happened meanwhile.

Mr Freddie Kingham, after a fruitless endeavour to soften the hearts of those at Scotland Yard, had returned to Camberley.

Mr Joshua Kingham had spent the previous night pub-crawling, and when Freddie returned he was in bed. Freddie rang for Bennet. But Bennet also was in bed.

Bennet, decided Freddie Kingham, who was more inclined to believe his uncle than the servant, would have to get up. He sent Browning, but Browning reported that Bennet's door was locked. More determined than ever, Freddie Kingham discovered a master key to the bedroom, and unlocked the butler's door.

He pushed it open and stepped inside, and then his fingers tightened spasmodically about the handle. The blood ebbed from his face, and once again he was seized with the need to be violently sick.

Browning, peering over Freddie's shoulder, saw that Bennet had been shot through the head.

* * *

Kerr, hobbling on one foot and a stout stick, returned from Bennet's bedroom some two hours after the discovery. The local police had locked and guarded the door until the arrival of the Department Z man, and Kerr had seen exactly the same thing as Freddie Kingham. With more experience, if not with less distaste, he had entered the room and made several discoveries that could only be called interesting.

Dodo Trale had come down with Kerr and Lois. When Kerr reached the morning room, Lois was saying to young Kingham:

'We would like to see your father, Mr Kingham. Is he in?'

'Why yes – that is, he's supposed to be in bed. *God*!'

The awful thought that his father might be in the same position as Bennet – for it seemed to be his luck to discover nothing but dead bodies – sent Freddie, closely followed by Dodo and Lois – scurrying from the room. Kerr watched them go, ruefully. Had he had two usable legs he would have been at Joshua Kingham's door yards ahead of the others.

But there were several things he could think about, and Craigie to be telephoned. He lifted the receiver confidently.

'I think Horn's cleared, Gordon.'

'How is that?'

'This fellow Bennet was shot through the mouth, and a ·32 automatic with his fingerprints is by the bedside. No doubt at all. On his dressing-table he left the usual suicide note – with explanations.'

'So it was Bennet, was it?' Craigie, Kerr knew, was not greatly surprised.

'It looks like it,' said Kerr cautiously. 'According to the letter he was approached on Sunday when he was at a pub, by a very tall fellow – obviously Kryn. He was told that the police would probably arrest Matthew Horn, but in any case when they came again from London, he was to hand that envelope and the notes – with forged initials – to Kingham. Apparently Kryn knew Freddie could not keep it from us. The payment was a hundred pounds. Bennet's been betting – I'll check up on that – and badly needed the money. Everything went off as planned, except his conscience.'

'Hmm,' said Craigie.

'Apparently when Bennet realised the spot he had put his employer in, he couldn't stand it. He's also several hundred in debt, so he took the easy way out.'

'Hmm,' said Craigie again, a little doubtfully. 'Will you check the betting and the debts?'

'Yes, before I leave. On the face of it, though, we can't hold Horn.'

'We can watch him,' said Craigie. 'Well, get back as soon as you can, and mind that ankle. I've just had a wire from Loftus – he's arrived all right.'

'Don't you mean Schmidt?' murmured Bob Kerr, as he closed down.

While Kerr had been talking to Craigie, Lois, Dodo and young Freddie Kingham had been compelled again to use a master-key, and for some seconds Freddie had seemed likely to faint. But no grisly sight met their eyes. The bed had not been slept in, but there were signs of hurried packing. No message was left behind, but it was clear that Joshua Kingham had flown in the night.

'I'm beginning to wish we'd paid more attention to Joshua,' murmured Kerr, glancing at several water colours that did nothing to help the harmony of the drawing-room's decorative scheme.

Lois's disapproving eye swept round the room and came to rest on the obviously flattering portrait of a man. Her attention quickened.

'See that picture, Bob?'

'It's not a picture, it's a blot,' said Dodo, scathingly.

Kerr screwed up his eyes and grunted.

'In other words it's a portrait of Joshua painted by himself.'

Lois said tersely: 'I've seen him before. At Rene Mondell's flat. He called himself Smith and offered her terms to work for Kryn – and you, Dodo, followed him!'

* * *

Dodo Trale had followed Mr Smith, or Joshua Kingham, to a studio in Chelsea. But Kingham, with the astuteness that seemed born in those who worked for Kryn and the Princess of Vallena, had managed to slip away.

It seemed clear to them now that the man they had seen as an indifferent artist, a useless wastrel sponging on his brother-in-law, was rather more than this.

But there was one thing still puzzling Craigie.

He had been telephoned from a Camberley call-box, and had assumed it was by the man controlling the Lane House end of the affair for Kryn. But about the time the call had come through, Kingham had been in London, with Lady Mondell.

'So there's someone else,' he said, when he visited Kerr that evening, 'although they might have gone there intentionally, hoping that the call would be traced. Does the Bennet affair really look like suicide?'

Kerr nodded.

'I'm prepared to swear it was, Gordon. There's no doubt that he was in a devil of a mess financially. The kind of mess that would make him do anything for a hundred quid, and when he lost that – he was ripe for a gas oven, or suicide of any kind. What have you done with Horn?'

Craigie laughed.

'For once I managed to get someone else to do it, Bob. Wishart saw him at Downing Street, apologised for the mistake, explained it was connected with Bettin's murder and stressed the need for absolute secrecy. Horn seems to have taken it very well indeed. He should be home in an hour. As our brighter men aren't available, I've asked Fellowes to put a couple of really good sergeants on him, and he and Freddie Kingham will be well watched. What time's your train in the morning?'

'Nine-fifteen, from Liverpool Street. We should be at Baj in forty-eight hours – unless you think we can go by air. It's not only quicker, it might be safer.'

Craigie thought for a moment and then nodded his head.

'All right. Once you're over there, you'll find emergency planes in the usual places.'

Kerr was more than thankful for Craigie's care. In most foreign countries agents of Z had arranged for private planes to be kept under cover, so that in the event of an urgent job they could be used promptly and with no questions asked.

'Right. Then unless there's something exceptional, I won't call you again.'

Gordon Craigie left the flat as Lois entered it. She was staying there for the night, in order to make a quick start in the morning. Trale had arranged to be with them at eight o'clock.

'So we'll be in Baj,' Lois said thoughtfully, 'soon after lunch tomorrow. I wonder – '

Kerr said seriously: 'Don't wonder too much, Lois. We'll get through or get put out, and all the wondering in the world won't help us to see which.'

Chapter 14

Baj

When Kerr's monoplane left the small private airfield near Heston, with Lois and Trale on board, it had an English registration and identification number. As it flew over the North Sea towards Holland, a Dutch numbering was substituted, by means of a sliding panel arrangement operated simply from the control-seat.

As the crow flies the flight from London would have been just under a thousand miles. Diverging from the straight course to take advantage of wind conditions, and again when they neared Vallena and were flying over the lower ranges of the Carpathians, they travelled just over eleven hundred.

Kerr was flying a de Havilland Comet, with a range of seventeen hundred miles, and an average speed of a hundred and eighty. As he had told Craigie, who knew little about aeroplanes, excepting their performances and possibilities, his foot was needed very little, and then only for the rudder bar. The Comet, in fact, almost flew itself, and in less than seven hours after leaving Heston, Kerr nodded towards the observation glass in the cabin floor.

'Baj,' he said simply.

Dodo Trale and Lois Dacre jerked into wakefulness. They had been talkative for the first hour, silent for the second and sleepy for the rest, and Kerr had decided that they needed all the sleep they could get – Lois in particular. There were moments when he wondered whether he had been wise to bring her: but she worked for Department Z, and she would be mightily useful. When he had urged Craigie to sign her on as a regular agent it had been understood that personalities must not enter into it: Lois was prepared to stand by that bargain, and Kerr could only do likewise.

It would have been better had he known a little more what he was likely to meet. But he was reasonably sure that he would be able to get on the trail of the man Kryn; and after that –

Well, as he had told Lois it might end either way, and they certainly had to be prepared for the worst. If it were humanly possible they would discover the real reason for the queer trade business, and the murders. If it was not, Kerr knew, it would be because they were dead: the issue was as simple as that.

As Lois and Dodo looked down over the rugged country of Vallena, two things stood out.

One was the silvery streak that wound its way in and out of the hills and ravines, and glistened an occasional gold in the sun. The other was the huddled mass of white-grey buildings apparently set at the foot of one of the higher mountains, and with a spreading, fertile valley in front of it. Neither Lois nor Trale had visited Vallena before, and Kerr explained a little.

'The river's the Pruda,' he said. 'Links up with the Danube near Galatz. Carries half that shipping we've been talking about, I shouldn't wonder. See the white star?'

He handed Lois a pair of glasses, and as she focussed them she saw the building that looked, from the air, like a white star. It spread in seven directions, radiating from a darker circle that she could not quite make out.

'What is it?' asked Trale.

'The Vallenian Royal Palace,' said Kerr. 'And the square block slightly north is Parliament House; the half-moon to the south is the Princess's home. Wonderful gardens down there – better, if anything, than the Tuileries or Hampton Court. I was over here for Craigie, nine months back. See that gap in the hills – the one with the white patch in the middle? That's our landing field. It's a private one, owned by the Pruda Iron and Aeroplane Company – and subsidised by English money. I wonder how many German fields like that there are in England? Anyhow, Craigie always keeps a plane there, and there are two other fields and planes within fairly easy distance. Just in case of emergency you'd better memorise the directions.'

Kerr went on brusquely, as though he was repeating a lesson and did not want to waste much time on it.

'Down here at the Pruda Company our man Sihilla is the Works Manager. Married an Englishwoman, and is pretty soundly British at heart. An odd-looking cuss, with long moustaches. At the north station there's Vincen, as bald as a coot, and with a dreadful nasal voice. Served with the R.A.F. in the war, and is managing a small aeroplane factory in Vallena now. At the south station you'll find Beltz. Beltz was in our Intelligence during the war, and he's convinced that the only safe policy for Vallena is friendship with England. Consequently he's still in our Intelligence,' added Kerr with a grin. 'Got the names?'

'Sihilla, Vincen and Beltz,' repeated Lois and Dodo promptly.

Lois knew that Kerr was concentrating on the landing field, and only giving them half his attention. She wondered why. Then suddenly she saw two monoplanes take off from the patch of white, and fly towards the Comet. She turned round abruptly, her heart in her mouth.

'What's it mean, Bob?'

But Kerr was smiling.

'One plane – get to hell out of here, it's not safe. Two – come down, you angels, no one but me is expecting you. It's the arrangement with Sihilla. He knew we were coming, of course. Best place to land. People expect aeroplanes, and they arouse no comment.'

Kerr took the Comet down smoothly. The land seemed to come towards them with a rush, and Lois shut her eyes. There was the slightest of slight bumps, and then the plane ran smoothly and steadily along an excellent landing.

Mechanics, looking no different from their counterparts

at Heston, were coming up with chocks. Kerr shut off the engine.

'Tuck your chins well in, in case there's a camera about,' he said. 'Ah, there's Sihilla.'

The man with the exceptional name was coming forward, his hand extended. Lois, who had pictured all manner of receptions at Vallena except this, stifled a desire to laugh.

Kerr made the introductions as they went towards the offices of the Pruda Iron Company. It was surprising how few people there were about.

Sihilla, using a sing-song English, explained quickly.

'They are *all* away, yess, Kerr? I send them here – there – lots of places. You no want to be seen, no?'

'You're perfect, as usual,' said Kerr, and Lois learned from that that Sihilla liked to be praised. He was in fact a vain little man in many ways, but exceedingly good-hearted. In his private dining-room he had prepared a meal for them that it would have been impossible to better.

It was half-past five when they had finished. Sihilla had fussed round them with the anxious solicitude of a landlady, but had not asked a single question. Kerr had asked plenty.

'What's the general opinion of the higher tariff, Sihilla?'

Sihilla pursed his lips.

'Well, well. Some say good, some bad. Always that way, yes. Those who like British goods – bad. Those who don't – good. How else should it be?'

'Who sponsored the bill?' asked Kerr.

'Oh-ho! Now you ask. Just the same, Kerr. Those who dislike England, yes. Prell – how sad, Prell – he was for it. Yes, very strong for it. The Nazi party, yes. They wish for all tariffs, up-up-up, but for German and Austrian. The fools! Against was the Rus-sian Party – the Socialist Right.'

That, Kerr knew, was exactly what Craigie had already learned from his men in Vallena, and it was not helpful. Apparently with the exception of Prell – strangely enough, seeing that he was Foreign Secretary – no particular man had been anxious to put the bill through, but the peculiar make-up of the Baj Government was responsible for the uncertainty.

The government was made up of four parts Nazi, four parts Socialist, and a fluctuating centre that, though numerically more powerful, might have been likened to the Liberals in England. The leader of the Liberal Party was an old politician, Nestal Silf. He had several times rescued the state from disastrous link-ups with other countries, and he was more trusted than any other individual. Silf was the Vallenian Premier, with a mixed party cabinet but a fluctuating policy. Had he been able to control his own section in the House the Baj Government might have earned more respect, but no one could be sure which way the Middle Party would vote. For some reason or other it had voted for the high tariff, but Kerr – as well as Craigie – knew that it might have done this for any one of a dozen reasons.

Until a week before, none of the other powers had, apparently, been deeply interested in which way Vallena voted.

It was a small country, insignificant, badly placed from a strategic position for attack, and of little use even as a defence. It had no substantial industries, but what articles of commerce it did manufacture were absurdly low-priced. The Vallenian worker was among the worst paid in the world. Had it been possible to increase its output it might have become an important factor in world trade, but it would have been unable, even if it had possessed enough workers to do this, to avoid prices going up with a bang. The chief quality of Vallena was its futility. It just did not count.

And now Kerr and others, including a strong body of English manufacturers, were beginning to realise that if it wanted to be awkward it might have a serious effect on English mid-European trade. And it was certainly getting that way!

Kerr saw one thing clearly.

The shipment of wrong goods had been done independently of Parliament. Firms had been blackmailed or frightened into doing it. Then, when English orders stopped coming, the Nazi Party had pointed out the fact, and the tariff had been put up. But had the Nazi Party been behind the whole thing in the first place?

The murdered Prell had been a Middle Party man, and the leader of the Nazis was a middle-aged militarist named Vonath. Count Paul Vonath, however, had always struck Kerr – and everyone who paused to think about it – as a sabre-rattling windbag. Could they have been wrong?

On the left was the Socialist Party led by the youngest member of the trio of party leaders. Meggel had a Russian mother, and that may have been accounted for by his Communist tendencies. He was the most hot-headed of the leading trio, and also the most transparently honest.

Kerr was convinced that the real leader of the ramp, the man behind Kryn and Cliff, was outside the parties. He was reasonably sure it was not Prince Renol. He was almost as certain that it was not the Princess of Vallena. She had been something of a beauty ten years before, the daughter of a wealthy Vallenian mine-owner. An impoverished Renol had married Katrina, his financial problems had been solved, and then he had turned for his pleasures elsewhere. Just what the Princess thought about it few people knew. Certainly most people felt sorry for her. And there it ended.

'And so,' Kerr said slowly, 'you can't tell us more than that, Sihilla? As far as you know, no one has been getting at Silf, Vonath or Meggel?'

'As I told Craigie – no one!'

'Did you hear any rumours about Doriennet and the others who were told to send the wrong stuff to England?'

'Not – not even – ' Sihilla searched desperately for the right word, and found it with a flourish of moustache . 'Not even a nibble, Kerr! Not – one – nibble!'

'Oh, well,' said Kerr. 'You've booked our rooms in Baj?'

'But of course, it has been done.'

A Packard was put at their disposal, and the trio were driven along a rough road towards the capital.

Presently Kerr began to swear.

He was driving, having refused an offer of a chauffeur, and he suddenly put his foot down on the accelerator as hard as it would go. Out of the corner of her eyes Lois saw something flying through the air, towards them. Instinctively she covered her face with her hands.

The Packard went like the wind.

Trale was watching the thing. It was perilously near – small, dark and round, with a wisp of smoke coming from it. It looked as though it would land on top of them.

The needle shot up. Sixty – seventy – eighty. A second seemed a minute and the waiting was ghastly. The bang of the thing on top of the saloon seemed inevitable. And then the roar came, from behind them. The back of the big car was lifted like a handcart and swivelled round. Kerr was helpless to hold it. The windows blew outwards, and Lois's eyes were dazzled by the blinding yellow flare that had come with the explosion. But in her heart there was the desperate fear so rarely away these days, a fear that they would crash.

The drop on either side of the road was at least five hundred feet.

Chapter 15
Shocks in Baj

No man on earth could have held the car. It went round like a top, sliding perilously towards the right, and deeper, drop. Lois was gripping Trale's arm tightly. She saw the rocky slopes of the valley beneath, yawning like the ravenous jaws of a beast as it waited for them. The car lurched further, the engine stalled, and Kerr braked slowly for the first time.

Touch and go –

Kerr knew the front wheels were almost over. They were moving slowly, agonisingly, towards the edge and a disaster that could end only in death.

And then Kerr started the engine, pushing her into reverse.

For a sickening moment the Packard balanced like a see-saw, over the edge of the valley. Then the wheels found purchase and it moved backwards.

Lois gave a high-pitched, hysterical laugh.

'We – we're still here!'

'Trust the old firm,' smiled Dodo Trale, taking his case out and offering cigarettes as calmly as he had done in Kerr's flat on the previous night. 'Not so easy to kill, even in Vallena. Take a cigarette, girl!'

At the same time Dodo wiped the sweat off his brow, and added that everything always seemed a damned sight worse out of England. Kerr was dabbing at his neck and forehead.

'Funny how they like working in ones. I saw the little swab standing behind a boulder, and he threw well and truly. At the speed we were going it would have been plumb in the middle and goodbye to us. But that's not the thing.'

'No,' said Lois, and it was a queer fact that all three of them forgot how near they had been to death in a realisation that the hoped-for secrecy of their arrival was a flop. Kerr's cigarette was burning unusually fast.

'Yes, they've spotted us. That's bad for Sihilla, I'm afraid. Dodo, feel like a walk?'

Trale shrugged.

'I never have, but I'll try it for once.'

'Cut back to the factory, and tell the old fellow what's happened. He'll probably have to get away. Meet us again in the Renol Hotel, Wilstrasse. All right?'

Trale took a gun out of his hip-pocket and another from his shoulder holster, glanced at them in turn and said that everything was fine. Between Trale and Kerr there was a quick understanding. Kerr hated to see him go, but Sihilla had to be warned if it were possible.

Lois looked at Kerr, who was watching Trale walk quickly and without the slightest appearance of nervousness, along the rough road.

'And what are we – ' she started, but Kerr moved so quickly that Lois started back. Kerr's right hand came from his pocket, yet it seemed still to be moving when he touched the trigger of his gun. The report was loud inside the car; but above the noise, a fraction of a second later, came a high-pitched cry.

'First blood I think,' said Kerr. 'Stay here, sweetheart, and if anyone comes either way, yell for me.'

He did not give her a chance to make any other suggestions, but hopped out of the car, and swung towards the wounded man and Dodo Trale, who had turned back at the sound of the shot. They reached the man within a few seconds of each other.

It was odd, thought Kerr again, that the man was alone: and he remembered Fencer at Camberley.

The wounded man might not be a Vallenian, but he certainly was not English: the torrent of abuse that poured in French from his lips suggested yet another nationality in the game of high commerce. Kerr's French was more than good enough to pass muster and he spoke brusquely.

'Who sent you?'

The man's sneer suggested that he did not lack courage, and Kerr had an idea that he was dealing with a fanatic. A pair of dark eyes glared at him with hatred.

'You would like to know, yes?'

Kerr laughed and the sound startled the wounded man. Even Trale looked surprised.

'I'm going to know,' said Kerr, 'but it can keep.' He lifted his gun, butt downwards, and struck the man sharply on the side of the head. The fellow grunted and dropped backwards.

'I saw him behind the boulder, Dodo, his gun trained on you. Watch for others.'

'What are you proposing to do with the blighter?' asked Trale.

'Cart him into Baj,' said Bob Kerr,

It was less than a hundred yards to the car. He picked his man up and flung him fireman-fashion over his shoulder, making his way carefully over the rocky ground.

Lois was out of the car, and coming towards him. There seemed no one and nothing else within sight or earshot.

'Is he badly hurt?' asked Lois.

'You're too humanitarian,' said Kerr. 'He ought to be dead. But – no, he's not at all badly hurt. We might find him useful.'

'But you can't take a prisoner into Baj!'

Kerr pushed the unconscious bomb-thrower into the back of the car, used a handkerchief to tie his hands, and then grinned at Lois.

'You'd be surprised what you can do in Baj,' he said.

Lois laughed.

'The day-porter at the Renol works for Craigie,' Kerr added unexpectedly. 'We'll get this cove up to our rooms somehow. Loftus and Oundle should be there, and we might get something from them. I only hope Sihilla's all right.'

He spent five unhappy moments getting the Packard into

position again. Its nose was towards Baj at last, and they started off.

Between Sihilla's factory and the capital itself were five miles of rocky countryside. The road was poor, and if the depth of the drop on either side lessened, the rocks towered in places perilously close to the car. Lois wondered what would happen if another bomb-thrower or gunman was waiting.

They came suddenly to Baj.

Lois could hardly believe her eyes. It appeared to be a walled city. There was actually a gate – open it was true – separating the country from the city itself.

But there was one welcome sign of modernity. Fifty yards from the gates was a café and petrol station that would not have disgraced the Great West Road. Kerr drove in, without blinking an eye, and shot a spate of words at a one-eyed man who came forward. The one-eyed man promptly disappeared into the garage.

'What was the gist of all that?' demanded Lois.

'I told him in bastard Vallenian plus a bit of French and a spot of German,' smiled Kerr, 'that we'd had an accident, I wanted another car quickly for my friend in the back was hurt, and tell the manager pronto. But it's all right. We're among friends.'

'*More* friends?'

Kerr looked a little smug.

'The longer you work for Craigie,' he said, 'the more you'll be impressed by the organisation. Every vantage spot holds Craigie's men. Mostly he picks politically pro-British people. Occasionally money speaks and where money speaks we have to be careful because we haven't all the cash in the world. The owner of this place was subsidised by Craigie – another bit of tax-payer's money gone! Watch and listen.'

From the garage stepped a burly-looking ruffian Lois would have preferred not to meet on a dark, lonely road. He was scowling. His shock of blue-black hair rose upwards sharply from his forehead, and a three-day stubble covered most of his face.

Kerr put one forearm across the steering wheel and held his hand palm upwards. He tapped the middle of the palm with his other little finger. The ruffian spat on the ground, and then pulled his nose, sharply.

Kerr spoke in English.

'I'm in a hurry, One Seven One. I'd like a large car, and this fellow in the back had better be moved inside the garage. Will you get rid of your mechanics for five minutes?'

'Sartain, Number Two!' The garage proprietor took it quite as calmly as Kerr. 'They 'ave gone, most. Drive in!'

His expression did not change as he turned and walked back to the garage. Kerr pushed the gear into reverse. As he drove into the shed, the one-eyed man came out, taking up a stand by the petrol pumps.

The change-over from the Packard to a large cream Cadillac took them very few minutes. An English fiver changed hands. The ruffian and One-Eye watched the Cadillac out of sight. Lois was beginning to feel that they would not be so lonely in Baj after all.

'You told us of the other three, Bob, with aeroplanes: are there many more, besides this fellow?'

'We've five men in Baj, altogether,' Kerr told her as he drove under the archway. 'This fellow, the man at the Renol Hotel, a member of the Royal Palace staff, one of the Government minor officials, and a leather merchant. When we get to the hotel I'll give you a complete list, and if by chance we do get separated, you'll be all right with any one of them. Meanwhile, here's Baj.'

Lois sat back and looked about her.

She was impressed by the width of the streets, and apart from the white stone of which the buildings were chiefly made, there was little to remind her of the east. The people walking the streets – growing more numerous as they left the gateway – might have been in Paris or Berlin.

No one seemed interested in the progress of the cream Cadillac.

Here and there they would pass tall, imposing buildings that looked larger because of the inevitable white stone. Slowly she began to assimilate some of the characteristics. The windows were universally small, she noticed, and the roads themselves were cobbled. The inevitable whiteness grew monotonous, and she longed to see a dull grey or a dull red brick, or granite.

'The roads all seem to run at right-angles,' she said suddenly.

Kerr nodded.

'They do, mostly. If their politics were as sound as their town planning, they'd be all right. We turn left along here,' he added, 'and you'll find that square building we talked about in the plane. After that comes the Royal Palace, and then the Princess's. They're next to each other, with only gardens in between.'

As he swung left, a different sight met Lois Dacre's eyes.

The squareness of the street plans disappeared: they were in a wide circular road, not unlike the Place de la Concorde but on a smaller scale. In the distance, perhaps half-a-mile away, she could see buildings like those which they had passed. But on the right of the Cadillac, and with another road on the far side, was the impressive-looking House of Representatives.

The gardens, filled with multi-coloured flowers that startled her in their wild splendour, were the work of artists. She had rarely seen anything more grandiloquent nor more peaceful.

'The hotel quarter comes next, and we'll be able to unload,' said Kerr.

Lois was conscious of a tightness across her chest. She had a queer feeling that they were being watched, and she knew that Kerr was on tenterhooks.

Were they safe?

Certainly no car had followed them from the factory, and

only the wounded man in the rear served to remind them of the previous attack.

Kerr answered her thoughts, that had run closely on his own.

'Of course, the Kryn crowd over here is probably as illegal as it is in England. They'd have to watch carefully. One man's less suspicious than two, but I don't like things somehow. I – my God!'

He was looking towards a blue Renault, coming in the opposite direction.

'Head down!'

Lois obeyed, but not until she had seen the man in the rear of the Renault.

His height was obvious, for his head was almost touching the roof of the car. He was looking away from the Cadillac, and talking to a woman who struck Lois, in that glimpse, as being superbly beautiful. In the front of the Renault, next to the chauffeur, was Rene Mondell.

* * *

'Was it Kryn?' Lois put the question breathlessly.

'It was Lady Mondell anyhow. Look through the back, Lois, and see where it goes.'

He was trying, without much success, to keep the Renault in sight with the help of the driving mirror.

Lois spoke swiftly.

'The Princess's palace, Bob! It's turned in.'

Kerr pulled into the side of the road. Lois turned to watch the blue Renault. It reached the imposing steps of the home of Katrina, Princess of Vallena, and pulled up. A few seconds later Rene Mondell, the tall man, and the other woman climbed out. They walked up the steps of the palace, and as they disappeared Kerr started the car jerkily.

'Well, well, well! So Katrina's in it.'

They slowed down outside the Renol Hotel. Adjacent to the main entrance was the garage-way, and Kerr took the car straight in.

Lois, on tenterhooks, wondered how they would get the wounded man inside without attracting attention. Kerr made sure the fellow was unconscious, and left the car where it stood. No one approached them, but on the far side of a large garage a boy was hosing a car down. Lois wished he would keep his eyes away from them, but Kerr's voice was low and cheerful.

'Get straight up, darling, I'll follow you in five minutes. Room thirty, on the second floor. Stay there until I come, and if Loftus is there, he's got to stay too.'

Lois smiled with a certain effort and slipped through the side door of the hotel. A page-boy led her towards the lift, taking her as far as the door of Number thirty. She felt exceptionally tired as she opened the door, and stepped inside. By habit, she closed it behind her.

And then she stifled a cry on her lips.

Standing in one corner of a large room was a tall, very fair man, with rather too prominent eyes. She recognised him at once, just as she recognised the menace of the gun in his right hand.

It was Gregaroff Shirin.

Chapter 16

The First Big Step

It was a dreadful shock for Lois and she found it impossible to hide the fact. She had not had the slightest suspicion that anything like this would happen, although she had suspected, despite the ease of their capture of the man they believed to be a fanatic, that others had watched them along the road to the city. But that Shirin should be here, before them, proved that Kryn knew at which hotel they had booked. There had been a leakage of information somewhere, and for once Craigie's network of spies had lost a thread.

Shirin was smiling, very well satisfied.

'Come in, my dear lady. At last I am happy to know who works with our friend Kerr.'

Lois smiled in answer: in the moment that had passed since seeing the man, both her nerve and her poise had returned. Her one wish was to get at the automatic in her bag, but Shirin did not look as though he would be easily hoodwinked.

And Kerr had sent her up alone: Kerr never did things or took chances without a reason.

'It's good to feel you're satisfied,' she said, and walked to the easiest chair. She sank down slowly, casually, dropping her bag on a small coffee table near her. 'Oh, I'm tired!'

Shirin's eyes held a glint of admiration.

'So. Not, perhaps, as tired as you will be, Miss – '

'Dale.'

Whether he was doubtful of the truth of that or not he did not say, but his gun moved a fraction.

'Thank you. It is most pitiful that you come for a visit to this beautiful city, and then you are not allowed to benefit, eh? And so unwise of Kerr to use a woman. They cannot be made to stop talking, eh?'

'They have that reputation,' admitted Lois.

Shirin smiled, very widely.

'It is good that you understand. There are a few questions you will be asked, and if they are answered – well, I believe that the Vallenians can be most hospitable. Otherwise – who knows? But come, we are in a hurry, Miss Dale. Any time now, I have reason to believe, Kerr will arrive. He will be most shocked to find the bird flown, eh? Now you have rested, I suggest the door by me, and then – the fire escape, that is your word for it? Most convenient, Miss Dale. Please! Do not make the mistake of moving the wrong way.'

Two things came to Lois's mind.

She was in no immediate danger if she did as she was told, and Shirin wanted to get her away from the hotel. That might conceivably be Kerr's idea, too, but if it was, why had he not warned her?

She stood up slowly.

'What undertaking do you give that I shall be safe if I come with you, Mr Shirin?'

The Russian's eyes flickered: it was obvious to Lois that he had not expected her to know his name. But there was something malicious in his smile, and his too prominent eyes reminded her unpleasantly of the fanatic in the back of the car.

'It is hard for me to say, Miss Dale. On others than me rests such things as that.'

Lois stepped towards the door by which the man was standing and as she got near him she tried a shot in the dark.

'I see. The Princess has a reputation for being a good hostess, I understand.'

'The – *Princess*!'

She had flung more than a shot in the dark: her words had the effect of a bomb. In that second she could have dashed the gun out of Shirin's hand, but she resisted the temptation. There was some purpose in this she was sure, and she had no desire to damage Kerr's schemes. One of the troubles of working with Kerr was the difficulty of following his tortuous thought, but he rarely thought wrongly.

'That's right, isn't it?' Lois asked smilingly. 'Surely you didn't think – '

Lois looked at Shirin: but she was seeing a different man. The suavity had gone, and in its place was a flaming anger. He gripped her wrist, twisting her arm so viciously that her cheeks went pale with the sudden pain.

'Talk! Who told you that?'

She said coldly: 'Let me go.'

'Talk!' His eyes were blazing, very close to hers, and she could feel his hot breath on her cheek. The man looked a devil, but it was because he was afraid. *Afraid!* And if she stalled him again he would break her arm.

'Craigie told me.'

Shirin flung her away, and she staggered against the door.

'Get outside, you bitch.'

She felt weak, physically and mentally. The pain in her elbow was getting worse instead of better, and her stomach was queasy. She wished she had taken the chance that he had once given her, but it was too late.

Where was Kerr? Why had he sent her alone? What was the game he was playing?

She reached the iron grille fire-escape, and now Shirin had her other wrist, holding it tightly and forcing her down.

The Hotel Renol was built on a square, with a courtyard inside the four walls. Perhaps twenty people were there, but no one glanced up at them. To look at there was nothing unusual in two people coming from the same room.

She was walking downwards quickly. Once she glanced round, seeing Shirin's face tense as they neared ground level. He was desperately afraid of interruption, and her mind was clear enough for her to wonder why Shirin – one of the leaders, she had believed – should have acted the part of a plain thug.

If he got her away, she knew she could expect no mercy.

She shivered, despite the lazy warmth of the evening. They reached the bottom step. A narrow passage led from the courtyard to the street. She saw cars passing as Shirin urged her towards it. She glanced round quickly, desperately, in the hope of seeing Kerr.

And then an unbounded relief flood her mind, and the tension of her body relaxed. Doors led from the hotel to the passage, and from one of them an enormous figure emerged. Despite the almost shaven head, the short quiff at the front, despite the baggy, ill-fitting clothes, she recognised Bill Loftus, now Herr Schmidt, traveller in wines!

He was wearing large, round glasses that gave him an expression of perpetual surprise. Perhaps he was surprised to see them, but she doubted it. His expression did not change as he came towards them, blinking short-sightedly as he met the full light of day.

Shirin showed no sign of suspicion.

Loftus drew level with them, and for a dreadful moment Lois thought she had been mistaken.

And then, as he passed, Loftus shot out his right hand. It fastened round Shirin's forearm, jerking the hand from his pocket and the gun inside. Shirin's face went livid, and his cry rang out involuntarily.

'Right about turn,' murmured Loftus in his ear, the muzzle of his gun poking into the Russian's ribs. Shirin turned round like an automaton. Behind those absurd glasses Loftus winked at Lois.

'Lead the way, *fraulein*, if you will be so kind.'

In a daze Lois went back along the fire escape.

The rear door of the suite was unlatched. Lois again went in first, but this time she went more carefully, to see Kerr stretched out on a settee, his eyes closed, a cigarette between his lips. In a corner, bound and gagged, lay the fanatic.

'Look at the lazy beggar,' said Loftus, closing the door. Shirin spat out an oath that Loftus did not feel was suitable for a lady's ears. He clouted the Russian, sending him staggering across the room.

On seeing Lois, Kerr jumped up quickly.

'Lois, my dear, I had to take that risk. If I'd said a word you wouldn't have convinced Gregaroff that you were surprised.'

Lois rubbed her wrist, and Kerr saw the Russian's finger marks. His expression as he glanced towards the prostrate Shirin was not pleasant.

'I see. Well, two can play that game. What did he want?'

Lois explained the gist of their conversation, including the fact that Shirin had virtually admitted that the Princess was in the game. At mention of Katrina Loftus looked up quickly.

'*Who* was that?'

'The lovely Princess Kat,' said Kerr, his eyes narrowing. 'And that makes it look as though she's working on her own, irrespective of any political party. Lois – will you hop into the bedroom for ten minutes?'

The door had barely shut on her when Shirin was on his feet, facing the two grim-eyed, powerfully-built men who obviously intended to have no nonsense.

'I will – I will tell you! All I know, all!'

'Proceed,' murmured Mr Loftus.

'It – it is not much!' Shirin was wailing, terrified lest the others should think he was holding back. 'For a year – just more than a year – I have been working. Me and von Hauf and Criff. Adolf Kryn – he was giving the instructions, not until last week did I know the Princess was involved.'

'When you say working,' asked Kerr, 'what does it mean?'

Shirin waved his hands wildly.

'First – it was among the people, here. Like Doriennet. Making them ship the wrong goods, yes, to England. Those who would not – we forced!'

'How?' Kerr knew, but wanted confirmation.

'We – we would threaten them. Frighten, yes! Once – twice – perhaps more – we sank ships.'

'I see,' said Kerr very gently. 'And were there crews on board those ships?'

'But yes, of course.'

'You had boats standing by, to pick them out of the sea?' asked Kerr.

'Certainly not! Why – '

Shirin suddenly understood the drift of the question, realising that he was confessing to the murder of a dozen or more sailors, who had no more knowledge of the reason for their death than a two-year-old child. There was something deadly in Kerr's expression then.

'I see. And you arranged this, I suppose, by placing time bombs on board?'

'It was not me! I was ordered. Kryn – '

'Why did you do it?' The question was like the slash of a whip.

'I – it was my work! I was paid to do it.'

Kerr waved the protests aside.

'All right. Your part was to arrange these things, and to put pressure on the merchants. What did von Hauf do?'

Just what von Hauf did was, it seemed, uncertain.

One of his tasks was to reckon the amount of trade that was being lost between the two countries. Apparently he did all the manipulating of figures himself; that might have been work enough for one man, although it hardly justified giving the German a prominent part in the affair.

'And Criff?' asked Kerr.

'Criff – he was so used to it, yes.'

'To what?' demanded Kerr, and Shirin looked towards the door, desperately, as though he hoped that someone would come in and save him from telling all that he knew. But the door was shut and locked.

'To – to providing – providing – ' Shirin was gulping, and then it came with a rush. 'To providing food, in times of war! All arrangements were for him, yes, he was the best man in the world for it, his business, it was the biggest! He had prepared – it is all ready! And then – then you found Criff. You caught him. Kryn, he was watching. He know that Criff says that Prell is working. To stop all other things being told, Kryn telephones – to the Princess. She arrange for the death of Prell. Kryn, he kills Criff – '

Kerr and Loftus stared at him, stony-eyed. Both men sat absolutely motionless.

It all went as they had expected.

Prell's death and Criff's had been arranged because Kerr had discovered – through Falling's death, which had not after all been futile – how deeply Criff had been in the affair of Vallena, and the effort to break off trading relations between Vallena and England.

But Criff had organised the provisions for war. *For war!*

Kerr brushed his hand across his forehead.

He said simply: 'What war?'

Shirin's eyes were more prominent than ever, and his lips were shaking and wet. The man's fear was genuine, and Kerr knew he was telling the truth.

'I do not know! Criff, he has been everywhere! France – Germany – Poland – Russia – all over Europe! You must know that! But where he has been working I was not told! I – '

Kerr stood up, and Shirin cowered back. But Kerr was smiling, if not altogether with humour. He felt a savage satisfaction at what he had learned.

'All right, Shirin. You're going to be looked after for a while, and afterwards you'll have to answer the Vallenian courts. I take it they were native sailors?'

'Some – some, yes! The vessels, they leave down the Pruda to the Black Sea, yes!'

'Right,' said Kerr.

He took a handkerchief from his pocket, and from another a small blue bottle. There was a reek of chloroform as Kerr leaned over the Russian. One convulsive movement and he went still.

Kerr replaced the handkerchief and the bottle. And then, as though he had suddenly remembered the man, he swung round on the fanatic.

He smiled suddenly and this time with real, if grim, humour.

The man who had thrown the bomb had seen Shirin's complete capitulation. Few men could have gone to pieces more thoroughly or with a more unnerving effect on a helpless watcher than Gregaroff Shirin.

In five minutes Kerr learned that the man's name was Vintelle, that he was a rabid communist with strong Russian sympathies; that he was one of a small but fanatical band of men in Vallena who urged Meggel of the Left Party to his wilder schemes, and that in this band there figured prominently the mysterious Mr Kryn.

Vintelle suffered the same fate as Shirin, after that five minutes. Kerr took up the telephone and dictated a cable to a small firm in London, apparently to do with the present state of affairs in Baj.

And some hour and a half later Gordon Craigie had a telephone call from the manager of the firm, and had the cable read out to him. He decoded it quickly, and read the gist of all that Kerr had so far discovered.

All within three hours of reaching Vallena, thought Craigie with a smile. And then he stopped smiling, for the news was serious. He telephoned the Rt Hon. David Wishart.

Meanwhile Kerr had gone to tell Lois it was all right, and found her stretched out on the bed, fast asleep. She stirred a little when he took off her shoes, and tiptoed from the room.

Loftus saw Kerr standing in the doorway with Lois's shoes, and grinned widely.

'That's right, old boy, begin as you mean to go on. I don't know quite *where* the polishers and shoe cream are kept, but I'll gladly find out.'

'*Very* funny,' said Kerr drily. 'Where's Oundle?'

'Gone to see the agents. He should be back any time.'

Kerr nodded. Had he come to Baj before Shirin and the others had left he could not have gained so much information. True, had he and Craigie acted more promptly they might have caught Shirin in London, but in London the Kryn outfit had seemed so much more efficient. Odd that it was less so in Vallena.

Probably, thought Kerr, because it was essential that no one should learn of Princess Katrina's implication.

He scowled when he thought of Shirin's finger marks on Lois. Damnable that he had had to send her up alone, but – there it was.

It had been a successful gamble, which was about all his work could ever be called. He had seen Loftus in the garage, as Lois had gone into the hotel, and Loftus had told him Shirin had visited Suite Thirty, by the back way. Kerr had therefore waited by the main door, until the porter had brought a message that Shirin and Lois had started down the escape. Then he had entered and waited, knowing Loftus could be trusted on the job below.

But he had to face two things.

First, the others *knew* about Suite Thirty, which had been booked by Loftus together with Suite Thirty-one, next door.

Second, Kryn and Katrina were obviously preparing for war.

He wondered again that Shirin *alone* had been used by Kryn. Why in heavens name did the blasted people always use a single man, where three or four altogether could have made the job so much more effective?

'I suppose we'll find that out, too,' he said aloud. 'We've made the first really big step anyhow. Now we're stuck until we hear something from Lady Mondell. Trale should roll up any time, and Oundle. Unless Oundle had been spotted.'

'Not like you to start jumping your fences, Bob,' said Bill Loftus crisply, 'and damn it, we haven't got to stick here indefinitely, just waiting, have we?'

Heavy footsteps were heard approaching down the passage and then a thunderous knocking on the door.

Kerr leapt to the window overlooking the courtyard and peered out. Four men, uniformed and ostentatiously armed, were standing at the foot of the fire-escape from Suite

Thirty. At the same time, Loftus opened the door. Three representatives of the Vallenian Military Police, headed by an officer whose trappings would have done honour to the principal tenor in a light opera, goose-stepped into the room.

Chapter 17

Under Arrest

He was a fierce-looking little fellow, and his sword rattled theatrically as he walked across the room.

With both hands in his trouser pockets, Kerr looked at him.

It might have been possible for a man to have shown more arrogance, but it would have been difficult. Kerr's: 'Who the devil is this man?' expression almost made Loftus laugh.

Three men stood in the doorway, which was left wide open, and stared blankly into space.

'Ho! You vos Rob-airt – Mac-*Mill*-an-Kerr?'

'Well?'

The officer's moustaches went upwards.

'Ho, admit it, yes! Excellent! You vos register 'ere as Arth-air – Brown?'

'Well?' Kerr was wondering whether it was worth showing force, then decided that there were probably as many men downstairs in the foyer as there were in the courtyard, and the odds would be hopeless.

'Excellent! You are und-air arrest!'

'My dear fellow,' began Kerr, but the officer cut him short with a magnificent gesture. Two of the riflemen with him goose-stepped forward, ranging themselves on either side of Craigie's chief agent. Loftus was beginning to feel it was damnably close to the end of things. They would be after him in a moment.

'This is absurd,' said Kerr, lighting a cigarette slowly and blowing smoke over the head of the fierce little man. 'I am an Englishman, travelling under the protection of – '

'Ze English – pah!' The officer spat, giving his opinion of

the English in no uncertain manner. 'You are undair arrest, for ze working against the int'rest of Vallena! You und'-stand? You wish to speak?'

Kerr laughed, and Loftus wondered how the man could behave so naturally when he must have been feeling like the devil.

'Not to you,' he said. 'Someone important. Who sent you?'

Why on earth does he have to put the fellow's back up? moaned Loftus to himself; it seemed plain silly. The officer's red face grew deeper in colour.

'The Kommandant! Ze Kommandant of ze Mil-arry Poliss! You will speak vit' him, pairhaps! An' you – ' He swung round and glared at Loftus. 'You are the great mis-take! This man, he is ze spy! You – you are the travelsman, yes, for Germany. Germans, they are the goots. Ze English – pah! You know ze prisoner?'

Loftus took his cue quickly, and scowled towards Bob Kerr.

'Ach, I meet him here,' he said gutturally. 'I know nuddings else, mein Kapitan.'

The officer whirled his moustaches and smiled approv-ingly at the understanding German.

'So, you undair-stand – he is the bads. Ze English, they vould not trade vit' Vallena, they are all ze bads! Come!'

Loftus saw Kerr's eyes fluttering towards the bedroom door. One thing was obvious: the Military Police had come for Kerr and Kerr alone, knowing nothing of Lois. He had given up hope of physical resistance for the moment. Lois had been the bait once, Trale once; it was his turn now. Loftus would cable Craigie immediately, and look after Lois.

'This is absurd,' he repeated, 'but I shall advise the Kom-mandant of your insolence. Understand that.'

A clenched fist shook in front of Kerr's nose.

'Please to remembair you are undair arrest! Ze car, it waits. Come!'

Kerr was praying now that Lois would not show herself. If she was seen in the bedroom, it would suggest a connection that even this fat-headed little devil could not miss. Her shoes were by the bedroom door, and they looked three times as large as they really were. Would she sleep through it?

The two riflemen gripped Kerr's arms, but Kerr shook them off with an oath. The officer apparently decided there was no need to escort the prisoner so closely. Beneath his anger, he was beginning to feel worried. The man had shown tremendous confidence. That was the worst of the English, you could not understand them. To refuse to buy Vallenian goods – pah, it was the insult!

At least, Kerr thought, he would be safe from a pot-shot from one of Kryn's men. Kryn, of course, was at the bottom of this. But why arrest only him, and not Lois?

Kerr marched – finding himself strongly tempted to fall in step with the others – down the passage and into the lift. Those who passed him seemed to take as a common occurence the sight of a prisoner under the escort of military police. Nobody showed the slightest interest.

Outside, dusk was falling; bathed in a golden twilight Baj looked more peaceful than ever.

With two riflemen and a uniformed driver, Kerr was bundled into a waiting Cadillac, the officer sitting beside him. The rest of the bunch loaded a couple of Fords, and the cars started off.

They were fifty yards from the Hotel Renol when Kerr caught a glimpse of a spindly fellow, something over six feet in height, who was walking with one of the Vallenian lovelies. As the Cadillac drew nearer, Kerr caught the thin man's quick glance.

That was Oundle. Oundle would soon be with Loftus and Lois. This thought did much to cheer Kerr. If he could find who had instigated his arrest he believed it would be a help: after that who knew?

* * *

Kerr had been brought to the Royal Palace, but certainly not by the front entrance, and as certainly not on the first floor. In fact it was a basement, and it smelt. Was it possible that the word 'dungeon' still had meaning in Vallena?

It was the nearest to one that Kerr had met, and he did not like it. Apart from the smell, it was damp, and apart from the water there were rats. It was also dark.

Kerr began to wonder whether it was really happening.

He hoped Loftus and Lois would not embark on a foolish attempt to rescue him – not yet, at all events. Even in Baj there would have to be some kind of a trial.

Kerr felt the sweat cold on his neck.

Would there?

Hitler hadn't worried much about trials in Germany, and Moscow, in its earlier days, had been equally indifferent. And – war was in the offing.

Kerr began to wish he had not taken his arrest so easily. It was simple now to picture the heroics of making a break, and to imagine the effort succeeding. It was one thing to take it calmly and in the old-fashioned English way, and quite another to view it from a dungeon with little ventilation, and rats for company.

War – war – war was in the offing.

And Kerr could do nothing. He ached to be up and doing. The one consolation was that he had already advised Craigie of the situation, and there were several strong and hearty agents in Baj, alerted now to watch the Princess.

What was she after?

One of these blasted mid-European coups, of course. But backed up by someone else, and someone Kerr could not identify. Judging from the fanatic it was Russia, but that solution seemed too well-worn. All the signs of international politics were red, according to those who were not, and rigid right to those who were.

The officer's goose-step had been too Nazi to be true: the fanatic's fanaticism had been the same. Kerr laughed suddenly.

It did him good.

Obviously to undermine his resistance, the swabs had taken his watch. There was no better way of making a man lose his sense of proportion than by forcing him to lose count of time. Kerr had smoked five cigarettes, and tried to estimate twenty minutes between each one. Say two hours and a half since he had been thrown in here. Nine o'clock now, within half-an-hour of it, anyhow.

What a picture!

He had gone so far as to imagine part of his conversation with the Kommandant. He had blinded himself into believing that he could discover who had arranged for his arrest. It had all seemed so simple, coming in the car from the Renol. This evil-smelling place was an anti-climax that he could not properly appreciate.

Had Lois or Loftus heard from Rene Mondell yet?

Worse, had Kryn discovered she was playing a double part?

His thoughts began to get chaotic. He had had too much time for resting and thinking, perhaps that was what made him start pacing up and down the cell.

Obviously it had not been long empty. The rats were not shy. They scampered backwards and forwards, and they thought nothing of running over his feet.

He sat down on the only seat, a three-legged stool, and found the stench of a sanitation hole over-powering. The stool was chained to the wall and he could not move it.

He stood up again, going this time towards the door. Just a few inches of wood, reinforced with iron stood between him and freedom.

Supposing they forgot him?

Kerr laughed aloud again, and the harshness of the sound made the rats stop their scampering.

He felt tired, very suddenly.

He slid down on the stool as waves of fatigue swept over him. He could afford to sleep. He *had* to sleep.

The next thing he knew a hand was at his shoulder, and

when he opened his eyes he was almost blinded by the glare from an unshaded lamp in the corridor outside the cell. Three officers were standing there, and two riflemen.

Kerr stood up, dazed and unsteady. He looked from one fierce face to the other. The hand gripped his shoulder painfully, and he was half-pushed and half-carried out of the cell. Apparently they were convinced he was a dangerous character, and he had to fight to stop himself from proving it.

The temptation to go berserk threatened to overcome him when he slipped as he reached the door at the end of the passage, and a patent leather toe told him to mend his ways. He felt more humiliated than he had ever been in his life, and the odd thing that helped him on was a mental vision of a hatchet face, a man whose hair was going very grey and thin over the temples, but whose eyes at times burned with the fervour of something bigger and better than patriotism.

He kept his feet and walked stiffly onwards. The passage led into a large room furnished in the stark and simple fashion beloved of European military officials.

It was forty feet across, built on a circular plan, and there were five or six similar passages leading to it. In the middle was a long desk, and behind the desk a single man – probably the Kommandant of the Cells, thought Kerr, on duty. Two stiff-looking riflemen stood to attention.

Kerr was prepared to dislike the gentleman at the desk intensely.

In the first place he saw only the top of a head, for the man was looking down on some papers. It was disconcertingly bald, the shape, Kerr fancied, Teutonic.

Feeling the biggest mug in the world with his company of goose-stepping officers, Kerr reached the desk. The officers came sharply to attention. The riflemen grounded rifles. The echoing ceased and the man with the bald head went on writing.

And then, with a sigh that could be heard plainly, the Kommandant – if it was the Kommandant – put down his pen and slowly raised his head. The forehead, broad and shiny, came first. The nose, a rather indifferent nose with a slight bias to the left, came next. Then Kerr saw the lips, the square and solid chin. The eyes at first were narrowed, as though with weariness, but their expression changed. They were smiling, they were friendly, and the Kommandant pushed a box of cigarettes towards the Englishman.

'Ah, Mr Kerr. Sit, please.'

But Kerr was staring like a man who had seen a ghost. For he was looking at the face of M. Jules Doriennet.

Chapter 18

Rumbles of Revolution

One of the officers snapped an order, and a chair was pushed behind him. Kerr sat down. The Kommandant's word was obviously law. He nodded to the crowd round Kerr, and they dropped back. He issued a command in Vallenian, and the riflemen marched towards the doors and disappeared, leaving only two on guard and one officer remaining.

Kerr was getting over his shock.

Doriennet! It was absurd, of course. Doriennet was dead, he himself had identified the body. The resemblance was lessening now. It had just been the shock, the sudden impression of looking at a dead man.

Kerr was glad of the cigarette. The uncanny likeness worried him, and the friendliness of the man's manner made him suspicious.

'Well, Mr Kerr.' The gaze was humorous, almost benevolent, and Kerr had a feeling that the Kommandant was genuinely amused. 'I understand you have upset Lieutenant Davos.'

'Davos? The man who came to the Renol?'

'The same.'

The Kommandant was smiling. What the devil was he looking so pleased about, wondered Kerr.

'You have no fears about getting free, Mr Kerr?'

'I can't imagine the Government so ill-advised as to hold me for very long,' said Kerr drily.

'No? You are, after all, a foreign agent.'

'You seem to think so. But foreign agents, in times of peace, are allowed the dignity of a trial, Commander.'

For the first time the other's expression of mild pleasure disappeared. He sighed, tapping a long cigarette – the Russian kind that Doriennet had favoured in Kerr's flat – on the edge of his desk, and sighed.

'In times of peace, yes. But you, doubtless, have heard the rumbles of revolution. Why else should you be here?'

Kerr shrugged.

'Aren't you assuming a great deal?'

'There really is no need to act.' The Kommandant's command of English was perfect, and his manners were more English than foreign. Kerr was beginning to think him a likeable man, and that had nothing to do with his probable actions in regard to Kerr: a man could kill you and still be likeable. 'I know you well, Mr Kerr. Craigie's men, unfortunately for him perhaps, are no longer able to hide with such secrecy. Some, of course, manage it. The better-known ones, such as yourself, suffer the inevitable penalty of fame. May I tell you, Mr Kerr, that until two years ago I was in England? That I was employed by the Vallenian Intelligence Department, and that I know your excellent record? I have sometimes regretted being recalled, but they say I am getting old. Tonight is one occasion why I am glad I am sitting here. I have often wanted to meet you.'

'Thanks,' said Kerr drily. 'In better circumstances next time, I hope. By the way, a lager – '

'My dear man, yes. Holst – *der laager*! Let us drop formalities, Kerr. When you came in and saw me, you had a shock?'

Kerr nodded.

'You are remarkably like – an acquaintance of mine.'

'Ye-es. Poor Jules, who died so unfortunately after seeing you, was my brother, Kerr. That enables you to understand a little?'

'A lot, Doriennet. I'm – sorry.'

'About Jules? It was, I suppose, inevitable. If the poor fellow had only told me, instead of trying to deal with it himself – well, a great deal might have been done. As it is, we are in an unfortunate position, you no more than I. I have mentioned the rumbles of revolution. They are distressingly near. Every time the door opens I wonder whether it is to announce the new order of things. As a military man, of course, I will be assumed to support the ruling Government. If it is a peaceful revolution – that might be – all will be well. But I am afraid of trouble, Kerr, just as you are. I cannot imagine how Vallena will avoid it now. Things have reached too bad a pass.'

Kerr shrugged his shoulders.

'You doubtless know more about it than I.'

'Yes. Your point of interest lies only in the effect on England, of course. Well, now. A word of explanation. A statement was made to the effect that you were plotting against the Government. The alleged facts were too grave for us to do anything but order your arrest. And now I am in the peculiar position of having to ask one of my political prisoners for information. You understand, I am sure?'

The vague pictures of third degree that had flitted through Kerr's mind when he had been shut in the cell returned. This had gone on far too smoothly.

'Sorry, Doriennet. But – supposing I don't, or can't, answer? What happens?'

Doriennet waved his hands.

'I had not considered the possibility, Kerr. I give you my assurance that I have one thing in mind only: to stop the revolution. I have discovered many of the people who are working for it. I know that the whole Meggel Party is ready to take up arms. I know that Count Vonath's Nazi group will jump into a battle as quickly. The revolution waits only for the match. Politics are hotter here than in England – but you hardly need telling that. The Communist and Nazi element has been straining at the leash for years. Unless we can act quickly we shall have a repetition of the Austrian trouble, after Dolfuss. Perhaps a repetition of Spain, with the added difficulty of Russia and Germany being very close to us. Germany, of course, virtually possesses a corridor through Poland to Vallena, just as they have at Danzig. Well – '

He broke off, inquiring, inviting. Kerr was trying to convince himself that the man was wholly sincere. Certainly he was Doriennet's brother, and the revolutionaries – if the break came – had murdered Jules Doriennet.

'Well – what exactly do you want to know, Komandant?'

Doriennet smiled, quickly.

'Excellent! I had imagined, Kerr, you would not allow your rough handling to prejudice you. One forgets oneself in these things. Well – I have discovered small arms factories, and broken them. I have found ammunition dumps and confiscated them. A dozen, perhaps, in all. I know that your countryman, Criff, was in it. I know that Prell was mixed up in it. All these things have come to light since Prell's assassination. But – I do not know who is behind it, and I must. The three party leaders? I do not think so. Meggel will fight, but he is a fanatic. Paul Vonath is a shouting fool. Nestal Silf, if not a genius, is a diplomat, and a true diplomat these days wishes for peace. So it is someone outside. Some country. Which one, Kerr?'

Kerr was very wideawake now.

'Which one – I'd like to know, too, Kommandant. But you talk as though you are sure it *is* an outsider.'

For the first time Kerr saw anger in those smiling blue eyes.

'Kerr! I had assumed you would talk – '

So he had no idea of Katrina, Kerr thought slowly. The man was genuine. He was friendly towards Kerr: he was an ex-spy, and he knew that Kerr and Craigie worked for peace. He was on Kerr's side.

'I've just decided that I will talk,' said Kerr slowly, 'but I'll repeat the question: you're sure it's someone outside?'

'Ach, it must be!'

Kerr was nodding slowly.

'In a way, yes. But the mainspring is here. The Prince, Doriennet?'

The Kommandant had pushed his chair back, and was now leaning forward and gripping his desk with both hands.

'The Prince – madness! He is weak, he is hated. No one would follow the Prince. Vonath, Meggel, Silf, they all have their supporters, but the wastrel Renol – no one!'

Kerr said very slowly: 'Is there any other personality connected with the throne who might win public favour? Who might get supporters from the army, the police, from all parties? As if, for instance, Renol was popular and wanted to set up a dictator state, with himself as dictator? Can you think of anyone?'

Doriennet was staring, his eyes very prominent.

'Kerr – you *know* something. You know. The – Princess?'

'I think,' said Kerr, 'that I can very nearly prove it. Listen, Doriennet – '

He talked quickly, for five minutes. He knew that Doriennet was incredulous at first, but was slowly convinced. He learned afterwards that Kryn was the Princess's personal adviser, he knew of course that Katrina had travelled all over the world, and that year she had spent a great deal of time in the Tyrol.

'Accessible,' exclaimed Doriennet excitedly, 'to both Russia and Germany. She is in the pay of one or the other! She can win the people for they love Katrina. She has been badly treated, so they are her friends. Even I – But, Kerr, there must be something else!'

'There probably is something else,' said Kerr, 'but Katrina's leading it here.'

He heard the running of feet outside, and saw the riflemen jump towards the doors. A word was shouted, another came from the opposite side of the door.

The door was unlocked, and Kerr and Doriennet, on their feet, saw the fierce-looking Lieutenant Davos burst in. Davos with his uniform torn almost to ribbons; Davos with a wicked wound over his right eye; Davos whom Kerr admired in that moment.

'Kommandant – it has come! The revolution! They are attacking the Palace! They are firing at the House of Representatives! They are mad, Kommandant, it is the end of all!'

* * *

It had come.

The revolution in Vallena that Kerr and Craigie had foreseen and so desperately tried to stop. That Doriennet had foreseen and worked against. That the three parties of the House had been half-afraid to face and yet half-welcomed.

It was happening.

The next five minutes passed like a nightmare to Kerr, a crazy kaleidoscope of the impossible. Davos had seemed to forget the Englishman was a political prisoner, had run alongside him, with the Kommandant and two riflemen slightly ahead. Kerr had had time to get his automatic from Doriennet's desk, and more than time to wonder whether the rabble had got as far as the Hotel Renol.

As they hurried up a wide flight of stairs they heard an occasional rifle shot, while in the background was a murmuring, like distant thunder, and the sharp *tap-tap-tap* of a machine-gun.

Kerr had no time to notice the spaciousness of the main hall of that section of the star-shaped castle, its tapestries, its magnificent furniture. He saw the crowd of men by the doors and the rough barricade that had been thrown up. Men were still working on it, and behind a priceless settle a machine-gunner was entrenched, pouring lead into the attacking forces.

There would be no peaceful revolution in Vallena.

The darkness beyond was speckled with the flashes from rifles. Bullets were humming over their heads. The crowd facing them was a jumbled mass of yelling people, the only light coming from the guns and a few hand-torches – an inevitable insignia of rabble rebellion.

Kerr reached the barricade, and as he did so a man leaning over it, his rifle at his shoulder, yelled once and dropped backwards. Another man took his place. Slowly, as the machine-guns raked the courtyard, the crowd was being driven back.

But for how long?

The revolt must have spread like wild-fire, and Kerr knew it was no exaggeration to say that it had been smouldering for years. It had come, of course, as a clash of Nazi versus Communist, but it went deeper than that, and Katrina was directing it.

Who was directing Katrina?

And how would England be affected?

And – Lois. How was she?

Davos could only tell them that he had been off-duty but in uniform, when the crowd had raided the café he had been sitting in, and he had fled for his life. Police, military, anyone who refused to help the rebel forces had been slaughtered – his words came incoherently, starkly informing Kerr of the bloodshed that had come to the stricken city like a plague.

Kerr turned to Doriennet.

'I've got to get out!'

'But how can you?'

'There must be a way, back entrance, a window. I can't stay here, I've told you all that I know.'

'I am not asking for more – but how – '

Kerr swung round. Doriennet was making a desperate bid to pit fifty against a crazy multitude, he could do no more. Kerr must act on his own. He was confused with thoughts of Lois, and the less personal issue of what and who was the power behind this revolution.

A German corridor to Russia? Vallena over-run with the armies of both countries: the long-threatened war which, in the end, no one could keep out of, a war ruinous to British interests, to sanity, to civilisation. The mad dogs had started, how could they be stopped?

Kerr was racing up another flight of steps. He met no one,

wanted to meet no one. He could hear the roar through the open windows, and suddenly, just in front of him, a brick crashed through a large pane of glass. It showered over him but left him unmarked, and he flattened himself against the wall.

The rabble was filling the courtyard of the palace, up to now held at bay by a thin line of military. The crackle of gunfire came plainly, the flares more brilliant, the roar deeper. He looked out on the heads of that seething mass, saw men and women alike moving to the insensate impulse of their fury.

To the west he could see the 'islands' of the hotel quarter. The roads were blocked by the screaming masses, cars were overturned, here and there one was blazing, its red glare flaring to the skies.

The neon lighting of the Hotel Renol – the hotel of the King whose palace they were attacking, whose blood they wanted – showed up clearly. Kerr moved on.

At every third window he peered out. There must be a way of getting down, of mixing with the crowd. An individual would be lost in them, if once he could get there.

He stopped suddenly.

He heard the roar of a cannon that seemed to detonate inside the palace itself, and as he looked out of the window he saw a space cleaved among the masses. He saw worse, humanity tossed to the air like so many scraps of cloth. Shrieks and screams replaced what had been but a menacing roar.

The gun came again.

The shell split them asunder, sent them rushing back, crowding away from the part of the palace he was in. Someone just below him was firing a nine-pounder.

But the crowd at the back still pushed forward. The gun-crew must have been well-hidden, for the boom of the gun came again, but the fighting was growing fiercer. Grenades were being thrown like tennis balls. There was the crash of falling masonry, another boom.

A roar, the like of which Kerr had never heard in his life, came, and an explosion that smashed every window in sight. The floor under him seemed to sink. Kerr had a desperate fear that he was falling – falling.

The floor held, but bricks had fallen from the walls. The rabble had found the ammunition of the nine-pounder below, and now that the gun was silenced they were surging forward.

There was nothing he could do to help, little to save himself.

He peered out, careless now of being seen.

The rebels were streaming towards the breach in the walls, and Kerr saw the gaps in the masonry close to him, and a pipe leaning drunkenly away from the wall.

If they got in and found him it would be the finish. He had to get out.

He climbed out the window, reaching towards the drainpipe. It sagged sickeningly, but by keeping his toes against the walls, it bore him. Beneath him the crowd was like a sea of infuriated madmen – but no one looked up.

Kerr scrambled down, his heart in his mouth. Ten yards, Eight. Six –

A bullet pecked into the wall beside him, and he knew he had been seen. Another struck close to his hand, a brick glanced off his shoulder, but immediately beneath him the people were rushing through the breach.

Four yards – and Kerr jumped.

He had no idea whether the people he would jump on knew he was there, but he was hoping desperately that those who had sighted him were further away. His foot crashed on a shoulder, a man swore, Kerr staggered against three others and sent them reeling back, cleaving a passage. He jumped into it, but people were grabbing at him, he heard the ugly yell of: '*Renol – Renol*!'

They wanted the Prince.

They had seen Kerr coming from the Palace and by God, if they got him they would tear him to pieces.

Hands shot out, ugly, demoniac faces loomed in front of him. Kerr was fighting, kicking, but they were all round him, the odds were hopeless, and he knew despair. He had his head well down and his fists were working like battering rams, but they were on him, ravenous for blood. He heard a loud roaring in his ears, something that sounded unnatural and horrible, and then he was swept off his feet.

Chapter 19

Came Chaos

The first bomb dropped fifty yards from Kerr.

The mob had hardly realised what was coming; frenzy had made them unconscious of anything but the storming of the Palace and the man they wanted to kill. They were men and women, ordinary decent human beings temporarily filled with a madness fostered, insidious, vicious and damning.

Kerr was beyond philosophising. He was thinking of nothing but the pain in his wrists, the blood on his lacerated knuckles, the thunder in his ears. And then, as he seemed lifted off his feet for a second time, an odd thing happened.

But for that roaring, most distant now, there was silence.

There was no shouting and screeching, no cracking of shots. Silence that seemed heightened and not decreased by the roar from the skies.

And then the explosion.

Kerr did not know what it was even then. It echoed in his ears, seeming to shake the ground on which he was lying. Almost unconscious, he lay there, unmoving. The voices had surged back again, but now they were shrill with panic. The rabble was running.

The second boom came.

He knew what it was then. He saw the whole thing. The bomb struck, and burst. The flame was a lurid yellow-red flare, and smoke shot out, darkening the already gloomy skies. And then the top of the doomed building began to disintegrate. It toppled slowly, sickeningly. About its base thousands of people struggled to find shelter.

Kerr was getting to his knees unsteadily when the third

bomb fell. He saw it like a man who was seeing something on a film. It could not be happening.

It was.

He saw people literally buried in tumbling masonry, men running from the terror and falling beneath it. He saw a woman – no more than a girl – with her dress torn at the shoulder and hanging from her waist, with a smear of blood across her face – and he saw a crooked girder falling towards her. She was running with the very fear of death at her heels, and death struck before she could evade it.

Kerr wiped his hand across his brow. Both were wet with blood. He looked away from the frightened, screeching mass of people, shocked by the suddenness of the terror from the air.

There were ten planes, all clearly outlined in the star-decked sky. They were well past the Palace now, but their instruments of death were still falling, while from the building which had been struck flames were shooting viciously, and the cries of the stricken were coming louder, more terribly to his ears.

Turned from rabble to rabble: from blood-lust to dreadful fear. Men and women were gibbering and shrieking. Pitiful wrecks, broken irredeemably.

Kerr lurched to his feet. From somewhere, God knew how, men in uniform were springing. A peaceful uniform with the badge of the Red Cross on the armlets.

Kerr went forward, to help.

The picture of Lois had to be forced away. He had to do what he could.

He saw three men trying to lift a girder pinning down five or six women. He went forward at a weak double, and his added weight brought the girder off. Then he forgot that he was Bob Kerr, forgot Craigie, Lois, everything but the desperate need these people had for help.

He was running with sweat, and his sleeves were blood-soaked to the elbows as he toiled on.

There was a lull. More helpers arrived and there was less

need of amateur intervention.

He had no idea how long he had been there, how long it was since he had left the prison. Kommandant Doriennet, Davos, the first news of the rebellion, all seemed a long way off. There were still sounds of the roaring of voices, but distant. Here and there the gloom was illuminated by the ominous red flare of fires.

Kerr stood up shakily, and made towards the hotel quarter. He told himself now that he had been wrong, he should have gone to Lois first, should have made contact with the other agents, although God knew he was useless enough. Useless?

That spirit in Kerr that so often made him attempt the impossible, stirred again. This was only the start. It could get worse. This was one city, a city of the dead; supposing it had happened all over Europe? It was the thing called modern war, and could happen in London, Paris, Berlin, Prague, Rome –

Kerr's head was clearing. There was work to do and he had to do it. He wished more than ever that he had not stopped in that work of rescue. One man made little difference. Better that a hundred died tonight than a million tomorrow; tomorrow, if this started universally, could last forever.

The centre of the city had attracted the rebels first, and the bombs that had been dropped went right across it. Who had ordered those planes? Who had –

But the thing had to be stopped, somehow. *Somehow.*

On every side he saw more evidence of the uprising. Fires were everywhere, and at some of the bigger houses looting had started.

He was walking faster now. Not a car on all four wheels stood in the roadway. Some were burning, others were smashed and wrecked by the tearing hands of the mob, the mob *someone* had let loose.

The Renol – oh, God, the Renol.

Its neon sign was still flaring. He drew nearer, and he saw

a dozen men and women entering. Ragged, bestial-looking, still maddened.

Kerr quickened his step.

Inside, the attendants and commissionaires had made no attempt at resistance. There were signs – though not very violent ones – of looting.

Only looting – so far.

Kerr went upstairs as quickly as he could make his legs carry him. He passed laughing, yelling crowds of the proletariat. A girl, no more than twelve, was cowering against the wall, terrified. Opposite her her mother was being pushed and jostled.

Kerr reached Suite Thirty.

He hesitated before he went in. What would he find? The place stripped by the mob, Lois –

Resolutely he pushed against the door. It was unlatched, the room was untouched. And in an easy chair, staring towards him with an expression of surprise, was the thin and spindly Oundle. A glass was in one hand, a cigarette in another.

There was a moment of startled silence, Kerr's more of relief than anything, Oundle's of stupefaction.

Oundle said in a reedy voice: 'My God, you want a bath!'

For the first time Kerr felt anger rising at the inanities of the men of Department Z. And then he sat down heavily on a chair and laughed. With a steady hand Oundle poured him a drink.

'Where's Lois?'

'She's all right. With Bill.' Oundle turned his head away as he spoke, but Kerr noticed nothing. 'Messy outside?'

'Looks like being messy inside soon. The mob's got the upper hand, and – '

Oundle walked easily to the door and locked it. With the same air of detachment he lugged a heavy settee and placed it in a position of defence. His strength was surprising, and he talked as he worked.

'Not for long, old man. The military's coming. Not a

doubt about it. Baj'll be under martial law in a couple of hours. Fact. Less, probably. Quite an army coming down from the hills. They're waiting for the air raid shock to pass, and then they'll cut through the mob like cheese. What about that bath now?'

'Don't play the fool,' Kerr said. 'I'm past it.'

Oundle grinned.

'I'm serious about the bath, you know. You can't possibly do anything like that, and I fancy we'll have to be busy soon. Shall I turn on the water? It was still running hot five minutes ago.'

'What's the matter with me?' asked Kerr irritably, and he eased himself up from his chair and made his way unsteadily towards the bedroom. It was difficult to understand why his legs felt so weak and his head so dizzy, for sitting down he had felt all right. The mob was still trampling the corridors, and someone tried the handle of the outside door. For a moment Ned Oundle had his hand in his pocket, but the rattling stopped and the heavy feet passed on.

'Spirit's going,' he said. 'They've had wind of the army.'

Kerr reached a mirror and actually stepped back a pace in surprise.

His hands were caked in blood, his coat sleeves were wet with it to the elbows, and there was hardly a square inch of him unsmeared. He pushed his hand wearily through his hair, trying to see the man beneath the mess. If Lois had seen him like that she would have given him up for lost.

'It – it's not all mine,' he said. 'I struck one of the patches where the bombs dropped. Turn the water on, there's a good fellow. There's a dark suit in the case. If you'll get it out and then come in, we'll talk.'

The thin man was unusually silent as Kerr did his best to wash the stains off. As he let out the third bath full of water he began to feel more normal.

'Well – where's Lois? And Bill?'

'They went off soon after I arrived,' Oundle said. 'Phoned through twenty minutes ago. They say they're out of the crush and there's nothing to worry about. Loftus got a clout, Lois escaped scot free. But if you're ready to take it, old son – '

Again Kerr failed to notice the significance of the sparing news Oundle gave him of Lois. Another time he would have seized on its vagueness, but now his mind was full of the assertion that the military were coming down from the hills. Why from the hills? That could only mean they'd been prepared for the attack and had been mobilised to come into Baj after it.

'What do you know?' he demanded.

Oundle sat on the edge of the bath and swung a loofah thoughtfully.

'Don't know why, Bob, but things came to a head today. Bill and I couldn't find much yesterday. Only talk of the rebellion. Just who, and why it was going to start, no one seemed to know. The two extreme parties were snarling, and – '

'Don't hedge, for God's sake! What's happened?'

Oundle stopped swinging the loofah, and looked serious.

'This, Bob. Meggel's party has been induced to revolt, the Army was taken out of the city, and only the military and civilian police were left in. Everything in proper order, no one knew why or what was coming. Word got to the Meggel crowd that the city was there for the asking. They asked. As soon as they got busy the military sent the bombing planes, and as if at a signal the army started marching. It'll be the bloodiest massacre since God knows when. The orders are to spare no one – men, women or children. They're wiping out the socialists in Baj, and then – ' Oundle was talking like an automaton, his face now deadly pale, as he contemplated the next twenty-four hours. 'Then – Katrina steps in. She takes over altogether, playing on two notes. First, the bloodshed must stop – and she puts herself in good with the Meggel crowd outside Baj. There won't be anyone substantially left inside. Second, conditional on the stopping of the killing, she puts the Nazi party in power, herself as dictator. She has Vallena where she wants it, so I'm told. Following?'

Kerr stepped out of the bath and reached for a towel.

'The murderous little bitch. Any chances of stopping it?'

'Can't see any.'

'She getting any outside support?'

'Money, as far as I can find out. Can't get any further than that, Bob, and damn it, I think we're wrong when we fancy she's after twisting the lion's tail.'

Kerr towelled his back vigorously. Now he was clean his bruised forehead and the slight cuts in his cheek, as well as a mass of red bruises over his back and shoulders where the crowd had clubbed him, showed clear and angry.

'You can't, eh? Nor can I, Ned, but damn it it's there. She's worked for the break with England, and Kryn was definitely out for Craigie and me.'

'I don't know – '

'Hand me those trunks,' said Kerr. 'The military force coming is entirely Vallenian?'

'As far as I've heard.'

'How'd you get all this?'

Oundle grinned.

'The pretty girl you saw me with is the mistress of Count Paul Vonath. Vonath was told what to do this morning, and of course he had to tell her. And she – well, it's a wicked world – told me. Well, how're you feeling?'

'Fine,' said Kerr. 'Where are Lois and Bill? Hiding out, or – '

Oundle gulped, and his Adam's apple was unduly prominent.

'Not so's you'd know it, Bill. It was Lois's fault. She's gone all proletariat, reckons they're having a crooked deal – and she's right – and maybe if Katrina isn't able to pull her tricks, it'll end differently. The Army's with the Kat, and so – '

Kerr was staring at him, his face slowly whitening.

'I – see. Where've they gone?'

'Kat's castle,' said Oundle quickly. 'I couldn't stop her, old boy, and Loftus seemed better company for her than I. Bigger somehow.'

'Kat's castle,' said Kerr, very slowly. 'Come on, damn it, what you waiting for? *Come on*!'

He had little idea of what to do, but he recognised one thing. Lois was right. The only way to stop the easy triumph of the Vonath and Nazi party was to get at Katrina. If she was missing, the Army would be at sixes and sevens. Kerr saw it clearly, and his admiration for Lois went up by leaps and bounds: and as it did so, his hopes for her safety diminished. She was in Katrina's palace. Kryn would be there with von Hauf and others.

Kerr saw the biggest political danger.

In Spain a Franco coup had almost failed, and brought Russia, Spain and Germany (and others on a lesser scale) into the firing line. Here in Baj, it would be easier for the Russians to get busy –

A Nazi state on their doorstep. Free entry for Germany and Austria. *Could* Moscow sit back and do nothing? And if the Russians really bared their teeth, dare Germany hold back?

A hundred to one against, thought Kerr, and he shivered. Criff had been provisioning countries for war, making all the arrangements. Katrina *wanted* to bring the struggle on, and if it came, England could hardly keep out.

Yet Britain, angry with Vallena, might stand aside. Kerr hardly knew what to wish for.

He was dressed and ready. Oundle lugged the settee away and opened the door cautiously. A couple of frowsty, dirty-bloused Vallenians glared at them ferociously, but neither Kerr nor Oundle wanted to precipitate a minor scrap. Moreover the frowsty ones were well laden with odds and ends of jewellery, even a couple of silver candlesticks. From below stairs the rumble of the revolution continued, an ominous background.

Kerr wanted to tell the poor devils what was coming to

them, but he hurried on. As he raced downstairs he saw things that made him wonder whether his sympathies were in the right place. That child was there, on her knees and sobbing. Across the landing lay her mother, half-naked and quite dead.

And then from the streets came an unfamiliar sound. Of marching. Orderly and regular and remorseless.

'Let's get going,' muttered Oundle, pulling at his sleeve.

Together they mixed with the crowd, pushing their way past. Together they heard the galloping close behind them, felt the surge of the crowd. And then the firing started.

'Down here!' Oundle darted towards a small alleyway, as yet hardly peopled. Kerr followed him. A hundred yards behind them the mounted cavalry swooped down, and the second massacre started.

Men – women – children.

The swords were flashing and the rifles and automatics crackling; the frenzy of the mob grew worse as it was ridden down.

Kerr knew that nothing could stop the night of horror, that Baj was a city of the dead.

It was isolated at the moment, but twenty-four hours could bring the bigger powers at each other's throat, and the danger in Europe had never been greater.

Kerr pressed on, grim-faced, the thoughts running through his mind as difficult to keep in place as quicksilver.

* * *

There could never be any doubt that the guards of Katrina's palace had been forewarned. The barricades were formidable and the mob had hardly touched it. Within a quarter of a mile of the scene of that dreadful massacre, the half-moon shaped building still stood quiet and unaffected.

'Lois got through,' Oundle said, 'by asking for Kryn. Do we do the same?'

It was astonishingly easy. They asked for Kryn, and were allowed to pass the barricade. Kerr had a nagging fear that he was giving himself up. He was here for two reasons: Lois, and Katrina. He had only the vaguest idea how to act with Katrina, but –

To his surprise the guards did not search the newcomers. Kryn's name was obviously all-powerful.

They went up the spacious hall, where Kryn had gone the night of his return from England. The guards knocked on the black door, before which two riflemen were standing. There was a sharp call, and the door opened. Kerr, keeping his hands in sight, went through in front of Oundle. He knew he might be walking into a trap, and yet –

He saw the last thing he expected to see.

Kryn. Lois, and Bill Loftus. Two or three higher officials – and two women. Two women in that room of black, two women dressed in black, their only relief the creamy whiteness of their arms and shoulders, and their Titian hair. Two women sitting behind a large, ornately-carved table.

The one was Katrina of Baj. The other –

They were not doubles. No more than the two Doriennets were doubles, but in a quick glance the similarity was startling. At a distance it would be easy to confuse them.

Katrina of Baj, and Lady Mondell!

Chapter 20

Four Against Odds

The black furnishing, the subdued light, the quietness inside the room, all increased the effect of a tableau. Kerr and Oundle entered. The silence was broken by the clicking of the door as their escort went out. Kerr had flashed a single glance towards Lois, and then he looked at the Princess.

Yes, she was beautiful.

She was staring at him, with her amber eyes unwinking.

'So – you are Kerr.'

Her contralto voice was deeper than average, but it had a musical quality. It broke the silence almost caressingly: and Kerr answered, speaking slowly, smiling a little and looking for all the world as though he were a foreign ambassador received in audience.

'I am Kerr, Madam. You sent for me?'

Katrina's smile widened.

'That is good, Mr Kerr. I knew, of course, you would come. In a way I sent for you, but for you to admit it – that is diplomacy at its best. You are, after all, something of what your reputation says.'

She was a match for him in words, Kerr thought. Perhaps, in more than words.

'Now that I'm here,' Kerr said, 'what can I do for you?'

She shook her head slowly, her smile lessening a little. None of the others moved or spoke, but Kerr saw that Rene Mondell's eyes were moving quickly to and fro. She was afraid of something, but Kryn, Lois and Bill showed no emotion.

'Nothing, Mr Kerr. I will not pretend that I have arranged

this for a discussion of business. Your activities make you far too dangerous. It is sad, but true.'

Kerr smiled widely, and the transfiguring effect had never been more marked.

'I'd heard, of course, that you had made arrangements for my murder, Madam, but – ' He shrugged.

'I am glad it failed,' said Katrina. 'I wanted to meet you. Your career in the air had my warm admiration, and when I learned you had joined the Secret Service, I was more than a little intrigued. I could almost wish that our paths had not crossed like this.'

'And prevented this meeting, Madam? For that, I shall always be glad.'

'Always need not be long, Mr Kerr.'

Kerr chuckled, and the sound seemed oddly misplaced in this room of doom.

'More murder talk? Haven't you killed enough for one day, Madam?'

He half-expected her to flare up, for that red hair bespoke temper. But Katrina seemed satisfied that she was playing with a powerless victim; her nervousness, if she felt any, had gone, or at least was well-hidden.

'Brave words, and to be expected. At least I can assure you, and your friends here, of a speedy death.'

'Aren't you forgetting that we are British subjects?'

Katrina's smile took on a tigerish gleam.

'So. It will be most unfortunate that you suffered in the rebellion that Katrina tried to put down, Mr Kerr. Even the new government can hardly be held responsible for the activities of rebels. You over-estimate the prestige of the English, of course. That has always been an English mistake.'

Kerr shrugged his shoulders.

'I wonder. Two can under-estimate, Madam. My cable to my headquarters, explaining the full situation and my own trip to the Princess's palace might make strange reading.'

Katrina frowned: it was odd how men and women in

high position assumed that everything would work out just as they had planned.

'You are too venturesome, Kerr. But you cannot prove that you reached the palace.'

Kerr laughed with real humour. Old friend bluff was helping him well.

'My dear Princess, I am not the only representative of England in Baj, nor are my friends. There are plenty of others. I was seen to enter, and by now the word will have gone out. My agents will be on the way, and the news will reach England. England does not always sit back, Madam. She has been tried a lot of late. Too much. She will be ready to act.'

He saw a different woman now. Her eyes were blazing with a hate that was close to fanaticism, and her hands were tightening on the arms of her chair.

'You fool! If England starts, she will be facing World War! Have you not the sense to know that? Have you not learned that Moscow is racing to Meggel's help? Do you not know what is coming? England – pah! She *dare* not come in!'

A little pulse was ticking in Kerr's forehead. The trick had come off this time: he had angered her and she was talking, but the news was going to be little use to him. He was here, but how he had ever thought it possible to get out was beyond him.

'A matter that the government can best settle, Madam. May I congratulate you on the thoroughness of your arrangements? A rebellion, a Vallena united under you for a day, and then an attack from Russia! And your allies? I need hardly ask. A triumph indeed for your Vonath Party, but I am wondering whether your allies will be as faithful to you after your country is sold as it is now. And I wonder whether you have contemplated the possibility of Moscow winning? It is so easy to assume the best, Madam.'

He was thinking as he talked, and the idea, conceived when he had seen the two women, so alike and yet unlike, was taking shape.

Katrina was breathing fast.

'How you talk, Kerr. You forget things, too. You forget how I hate Vallena, how the Prince has treated me, how I have been insulted and spurned. Popular, they say? Only because they hate the Prince! And in the new Baj, how shall I last? They will kill me, Kerr. They will assassinate me when the new order of things has come – those whom I am helping, those in whose interests – ' she laughed, mockingly. 'I am starting this war, Kerr. You are beginning to see now?'

'You take the words out of my mouth,' said Kerr. He knew now, of course, what she was planning to do.

She rose suddenly, in a single, superb movement.

'So. And I have made arrangements, Kerr, you understand? It will not be safe for Katrina to live, after this. And I care nothing for Baj, for Vallena. So – after tonight – they will find me *dead*. You see that? They will think I am dead, they will have no fears. But I shall live, and she – '

Rene Mondell was close to her, terror in her eyes. Kryn had his right hand inside his pocket: the two officers had theirs on the butts of their revolvers.

Rene said nothing, but she stared at Kerr, mutely appealing. The idea in Kerr's mind was growing apace.

'She will die, Madam? Nicely arranged! And her husband – you have arranged for him too? And you will disappear, one of the best known women in the important centres of the world? It will be monotonous for you to live in retirement.'

He saw that Katrina was in good temper again, and his brows knitted. She was laughing at him, the only moving thing in that tableau: and laughing, with her fine teeth showing, she looked the loveliest thing in creation.

'But no, Kerr! She has a husband, you must know. Sir Douglas Mondell, he is most accommodating. He really cares nothing whether he has the genuine wife, or – so you see? I shall take her place, as she dies in mine. It has all been arranged. And if people think she has changed – who should know better than her husband? Their reconcilation is all ready, for the English papers. The whole story – so. And I, Katrina, disappear. I am dead. I have money, money for myself and for my *husband*.'

In the silence that followed, Kerr tried to get the whole thing into focus. Mad perhaps, but it was feasible, and with Mondell's help it could work successfully.

Rene Mondell, poor little devil, the cat's paw.

'No. *No!*' She was on her feet, deathly white, but no one took the slightest notice of her. Kerr's eyes rested on Katrina, their expression beaten, afraid. The Princess lifted her hands with delight.

'You see, Kerr!'

'Yes, I see.' He spoke like a tired man. 'Well – it's over, I suppose? I can't buy you off – '

'So! Kerr changes his tune. And so quickly! I am a little disappointed, Mr Kerr.'

Kerr's face looked like death. Lois Dacre could not be sure whether in fact he was acting or not. She knew his ability, and she believed in him, although since she had arrived here she had been convinced that there was no hope for any of them at all.

'But surely you needn't be,' Kerr said. 'You have done everything you set out to do. The only thing I haven't discovered,' he added slowly, 'is why you arranged that absurd business with the English trade. Why upset England? Oh, it's not important – '

Katrina laughed into Kerr's face.

'Absurd, Kerr? Unimportant, Kerr? How little you know, how badly you have failed to maintain that reputaton of yours! The reason for the interruption of trade with England is simple: the Vonath Party. The Nazi Party, the anti-Moscow party. You see?'

'Just words,' said Kerr contemptuously.

'Words, you call them! Just words!' Her voice rang out, filled with triumph. 'You will listen to me! The trade is useless now to England. Your big financiers, will *they* wish to help Vallena, a country no longer important to them? They will not! They will be quiet. They will eat their words, they will talk of sanctions, of piracy, of small things, and Vallena will be over-powered by Moscow, which is so near, and Germany will wish to fight because Moscow will then be more dangerous, and England will stay out of it until one or the other has won in Europe, and then – '

Kerr's mind was working fast. The fiendish cleverness of the thing, the long-sightedness of it, appalled him.

She went on, her voice rising higher and higher.

'You see, if England had substantial interests here she would have to come in *now*. Without them she will stay out. And when Russia is overcome, how weak is England's position. Europe will be united, Russia, Germany, Italy, the smaller states, they will all be one. Only France might fight, and then England *must* come in. Too late, Kerr, too late! She could swing the scales if she fights now, but later – '

Kerr remembered England's hostility, her indifference, towards Vallena. It was the natural result of that careful, steady work to antagonise the two countries.

'Where do you come in, Katrina?'

She laughed, on a softer note.

'I come so well, Kerr. Adolf Kryn and I, we have been preparing, through Criff. We have interests, food interests, everywhere. And food in war means money, and money in peace means power.'

'In peace,' Kerr muttered. 'There won't be any. Tell me one thing, Madam. Does the Führer know of this?'

Her teeth were bared.

'He knows of the rebellion. He will seize his chance, as Il Duce will. They are great men, these dictators. They are fools, too – like the English. I, and Kryn, and – others – will have the control of food in the days of famine which come afterwards. You see how powerful we will be? You see why we did not want you and Craigie to learn? Craigie, he would see the Führer. He would show the records of what I have done, through the poor Criff, who knew too much. He would see them all, even Moscow. He would show how they fall into my hands, and – it would not happen. It would be a revolution in Vallena, nothing more. But now the chance has come to put Moscow and Berlin to fight, and they will fight! Moscow has promised help to Meggel. Berlin to help Vonath. I will be dead, they think, and – '

'Well,' said Kerr slowly, 'it's pretty big, I grant you. Knowing Russia and Germany, you stand an excellent chance of success. Excellent that is but for one thing.'

He was smiling at her now.

She was eyeing him, her eyes narrowed and her lips curling back. Kryn spoke at last, thinly, viciously.

'Send them away, Highness. You have told them enough, and time is pressing. You must be out of the city by dawn, and there are a great many things to do.'

Katrina stopped him with a lift of her hand.

'What is that one thing, Kerr?'

Kerr smoothed his coat lapel with his right hand. He glanced just once towards Loftus, trying to send a message.

And then his hand moved like lightning to his shoulder. holster.

'*But for this*!' roared Kerr.

He ducked as he fired. Loftus had pushed Lois behind him. Kryn and the guards swept their guns out, but Kerr's first bullet found Katrina's head, the second Kryn's shoulder Loftus was in front of Lois, his bullets streaming towards the guards, fire coming back both ways. Kerr felt one-two-three sharp jabs in his arm, but as they came he saw the officers toppling.

Kryn was in a crumpled heap, Katrina was across the desk, the blood coming from her forehead in an ugly trickle. There was a heavy banging on the door of the room. Raised voices could be heard; footsteps.

Rene Mondell was stretched across the desk, the mask of terror still there. Kerr jumped towards her, his left arm hanging limp. His right fingers bit into her shoulder.

'Listen – damn you, listen! Go to the door, tell them it is

all right – just say: *faita rienta. Faita rienta.* They'll think you're Katrina! You can do it!'

The din outside was growing worse. Kerr dragged Rene Mondell from the desk, with desperation in his heart: and then realised suddenly what might make her act.

'Falling died for this. *Falling*!'

It seemed like thunder outside, the voices were hoarser, only the knowledge that it was Princess Katrina's chamber stopped the guards from breaking the door down. And suddenly, when Kerr had given up all hope, sanity came to Rene Mondell's eyes.

'All right. *Faita – rienta.*'

Kerr let her go.

Loftus was dragging Kryn from the floor towards a corner. Lois was standing in front of the bowed head of the Princess who had set the nations at each other's throats for power and money. The officers were sprawled out of sight behind the door. When it opened the men in the passage would see only Rene Mondell – and think, please God, that she was Princess Katrina.

Oundle opened the door as Rene reached it.

She drew herself up, superbly, and the haughty arrogance of her expression was perfect. A big, uniformed man was there, halfway in the room. He saw Katrina and jumped back in surprise.

'*Faita rienta!*'

It was Katrina's nuance, Katrina's voice. The man saluted sharply, and muttered something in Vallenian. Rene lifted her right hand imperiously towards the unseen Oundle, and he closed the door slowly.

Kerr took a step towards Rene Mondell, his eyes gleaming.

'Perfect! They're off for a bit, but now we've got to get away. After we've phoned Craigie – '

He knew, they all knew, what would happen if the message was intercepted. But it had to be attempted. The five of them could die if it meant Craigie could be informed, and the work of prevention started. Kryn was dead, and Katrina, but Sir Douglas Mondell was in this thing.

And others.

Who were they?

Chapter 21

And Others

Would the call never come?

It had been nerve-wrecking as Rene had lifted the telephone and, coached by Kerr, asked for that familiar London number, Whitehall 12121-8. At the exchange inside the palace the number might be viewed with suspicion, Rene's voice might be suspected, the Vallenian pronunciation was almost certainly wrong. The exchange had muttered something back, and Rene had replaced the telephone.

They would hardly expect her to hold on while they were contacting London.

Kerr cursed the fact that there were no windows. There were two other doors besides that leading to the passage, but he dared risk no sorties until the call was through. He was sweating hard, while Lois was saying in a matter-of-fact voice:

'Your arm, Bob – is it much?'

'No, it's all right old girl – they just nicked me.'

'Did they?' said Lois tranquilly. 'Now just take off your coat, darling.'

Kerr shrugged. His shoulder was giving him hell, but he was aching to get to the telephone, a second's delay might prove fatal. He lifted his left arm a fraction, and it would go no further. He grimaced, and then looked with surprise at the blood seeping down his sleeve.

'Just a nick,' said Lois, her expression grim. 'Easy, now – easy Bob.'

Between them, she and Loftus had his coat off. The top of the arm was a mess. Lois had a small pair of scissors in her bag, and used them, cutting the shirt away. There were three bullet holes, and two had certainly hit the bone. Her lips tightened. Loftus made no comment. Lois took a scarf from her neck, and a carafe of water from the desk.

Kerr, half-occupied with stifling the pain and half with straining for the first sound of the telephone, was dead white. Lois had the worst of the mess cleaned at last, and exchanged a meaning glance with Loftus.

Then the telephone came, sharp and shrill.

Although they had been waiting for it so desperately, they all jumped. Kerr wrenched himself away, and could hardly wait for Rene Mondell to lift the receiver. She said something in English, after a pause, and turned to Kerr. Her face was vivid with hope.

'It's Mr Craigie.'

Kerr grabbed the telephone, and caught Craigie's slow: 'Who is that? Who – '

'Hold everything,' Kerr snapped, without introducing himself. 'Can you hear me?'

'Right, Bob.' Craigie would have picked that voice out of a thousand. 'You all right?'

'Craigie, listen – '

Craigie listened, without comment. Kerr was speaking quickly, feverishly, half-afraid that they would be cut off at any moment, while the others were looking towards the doors, guns in hand. No interruption came. Kerr kept hammering home the points, one after the other.

'It's a food ramp, no more, no less – can you see it? Can you – '

'I've got it,' Craigie said quickly. 'I'll send messages to the ambassadors in Berlin and Moscow, and I'll get Wishart over here at once. You're in time, Bob. Are you – '

'It's touch and go, Russia's waiting, probably on the march. It's cleverer than I can put over, don't lose a second, man. Not a second – '

At the other end, Craigie had the receivers off two other phones and was tapping messages in morse, asking for connection with the Embassies in the two big Powers.

'The calls are going through, Bob. But you?'

Kerr dropped the receiver and looked half-stupidly at the others. As far as he could do it, he had finished the affair. It would be touch and go, but once convince Berlin and Moscow that they were the tools in a wider game, and there would be no big trouble.

Loftus was grinning. Oundle was smoothing his wiry hair. Rene Mondell and Lois Dacre were, oddly enough, holding hands.

'God,' said Kerr, 'couldn't I manage a beer. Eh?' he laughed. 'Well, let's get through into those other rooms. Be caught in here if we're not careful. I – '

He broke off.

The others swung round, towards the door, for the tapping came very clearly. Kerr swallowed hard as it came again, sharp and imperative.

'By the doors,' he snapped to the others.

They retreated, a man and a woman by each of the far doors. Kerr took his second automatic from his coat pocket and went towards the passage door. His pulse was beating fast, he wished he had used Lady Mondell again.

'*Ontra!*'

The door opened slowly at first and Kerr, behind it, saw the man who entered. He saw the expression of stupefaction on the man's face, but his gun showed very clearly.

'Tell the guards to clear off!'

He hardly knew how he managed to speak so plainly, to think clearly. He certainly did not realise that the scared newcomer gave the order, entered – with Kerr's gun a foot away from him – and closed the door. The man knew that he was facing death.

Kerr and the others were staring at him, and Kerr was muttering his name.

'Horn. Matthew *Horn*, eh? Well, Horn – '

Matthew Horn advanced a step into the room, and saw the dead bodies as well as the English couples by the opposite doors. His lips opened and the cry started, but Kerr's fist caught him under the jaw. Horn staggered back, the cry unuttered. Kerr managed to stop him from thudding to the floor.

Horn was out, for the time being, and they needed him conscious. There was no water left but there was whisky, and they forced it down his throat. He spluttered and sat up, his face pale, his teeth chattering. Kerr, conscious of an increasing pain in his left arm, started to speak.

'So it was you, little man, but we can talk afterwards. Were you coming to get away with Katrina and Kryn?'

Dazed by the great blow, Horn nodded.

'How?'

'The – there's a plane – on the roof. Katrina's – sports plane. Waiting. But – but – '

'All things considered, you'd better lead the way,' said Kerr slowly. 'You know it?'

The gun moved forward from Kerr's hand.

'Through the main passages?'

'N-no. Through – her bedroom.'

'Where did they keep their papers?'

'They – they're packed. On top. All ready. I've just seen – von Hauf – up there. He's waiting.'

Kerr was smiling, very softly, as though he had seen the light: and this news was the best he had had for a long time, for it offered a chance that had seemed impossible ten minutes before.

'And a pilot?'

'No. Katrina – was going – ' He stared across at that bowed figure, and he started trembling. Loftus pushed the whisky under his nose again, while Kerr snapped:

'Remember the gun's very close, Horn. Very close.'

'Bob,' said Lois, 'you're all in. Leave it to the others.'

Kerr's smile was faint but his eyes were gleaming.

'Not used to it, old girl. I – oh, all right. But make it fast. God, how I wish Trale – '

'We can't worry about any of them,' said Lois quickly. 'You'll need those papers to prove the case, and you've got to get away. Come on.'

She had his right arm firmly. In a daze, Kerr saw Loftus poke his gun into Horn's ribs. In a daze, he followed the others through Katrina's bedroom, without noticing its lofty spaciousness and its luxury, to a small staircase that seemed to trip him up at every step. Up, up, up, he went, Oundle helping him, until the cool night air touched his face.

It steadied Kerr.

The roof was flat, giving room for a short take-off run. The plane was inside its white stone hangar, the plane of the playgirl Princess of Baj.

It was larger than he expected, a seven seater. Room for them all. Kerr wished Trale was with them. It did not seem right to be going back without Trale.

Loftus kept tight hold on Matthew Horn, that innocent-seeming partner of Horn, Beddle and Graham of Tooley Street, the man who behaved so well to his relatives. None of them could really convince themselves they would get away without more trouble.

The roof was high up, but not high enough to avoid hearing the sounds of the strife below. The military were marching, next morning Vonath would be in power, and waiting for the results, while Meggel's rabble would be smashed almost beyond recognition as he waited for help from Moscow.

Oundle was fiddling with the controls when Loftus heard the sound.

It came from behind him. He swung round, and as he did so a bullet hummed out. It smashed into the wing of the monoplane, but before the man lurking in the shadows could fire again, Loftus hit him twice through the chest.

He toppled forward, into sight. Lois saw that it was the pug-featured man who had once pestered the Brigade Captain at the fire at Devennet Court. He was lying very still.

And for the first time Matthew Horn seemed to realise

what was happening and what he was doing. He muttered under his breath, and Kerr heard the same name several times. Sam – Sam – Sam.

Who the devil –

Kerr realised suddenly who it was, but Loftus had left the man, and was in the plane – it had an automatic starter and the propellers did not want turning.

Freddie Kingham's no-good brother Sam, of course. He had been in it, with his father and his uncle. It looked as if Freddie Kingham was the only member of the Camberley household with a clean record.

The engines roared.

Oundle nursed them for a few seconds, and then eased off the brakes. The monoplane staggered as it took off, steadied, and then went smoothly. In a few moments the ravaged city was beneath them, speckled with the lights of a thousand fires. Horror beyond words was down there.

Horror they dared not think of.

'Seven hours, with luck,' said Ned Oundle suddenly. 'Hope the lady put petrol in for a long hop, if not we're sunk.'

Kerr jerked his head round.

'Look at the gauge, you fool.'

'That's an idea,' grinned Oundle. 'Two – no, three hundred gallons. Enough?'

'Nearly enough for there and back,' said Kerr.

'Back?' repeated Lois with her first sign of emotion. '*Never!*'

* * *

When Princess Katrina's monoplane was flying over Prague, some two-and-a-half hours later, there was sensation in Berlin. The news had come through that the revolt had started in Vallena, that atrocities of unparalleled cruelty had been perpetrated by the Communists, that Russia was sending a strong force to support the Meggel Party. Wires hummed, troops were massed.

At the same time, in Moscow, it was believed that the big chance had come at last. The revolt had broken out in Baj, atrocities beyond parallel were due to the Nazis, Germany was sending strong forces by air.

Had Katrina lived she would have seen her triumph, even though her scheme to keep England out of the first upheaval might have failed.

Instead it was Rene Mondell who heard what happened. It was six hours afterwards when the monoplane had landed at Croydon and the party had reached Whitehall, that the British Ambassadors to Berlin and Moscow had intimated in no uncertain terms that if Moscow would wait, proof would come. If Berlin would wait, proof would come –

Would sanity prevail?

* * *

Sanity, Gordon Craigie told them, was prevailing. With the papers that had been brought over, the whole record of the coup from its inception would be available for convincing both Berlin and Moscow.

'Thank God for that,' said Lois Dacre, 'and now you're for hospital, Bob. That arm must have attention.'

Craigie nodded.

He saw Kerr and Lois, with Rene Mondell and Oundle, go out of the room. He was left alone with Loftus – von Hauf and Horn were at Cannon Street – and he knew Kerr had been on his last job. Loftus was here though, young, receptive to ideas, capable, quick thinking.

The work had to go on.

It was four days before the alarms were finally over, and Europe settled down until the next threat of upheaval. In Vallena, neither Meggel nor Vonath had gained the upper hand, and the old patriarch, Nestal Silf, was restoring order. The bloodshed was finished, Katrina was dead, the truth was published.

There were various odds and ends for Craigie to clear up in England.

He learned that Matthew Horn had been the instigator of the ramp, but at the time of his arrest, and Kryn's attempt to fasten the blame for Doriennet's murder on him, Kryn had not known he had been working for some time with Katrina; Kryn had believed Horn to be an associate of Criff, and had planned to render him innocuous. Bennet's remorse and suicide had saved Kryn from a gigantic blunder.

Horn had put his finger on the one vital factor. With English commercial interests inimical to Vallena, pressure could – and would – have been brought to bear on the British Government to ensure non-intervention. Horn had known the powers of financial interest!

Indirectly – through Criff – Horn had put the proposition to Kryn, who had found Katrina an easy listener.

Horn had sent that telephone message to Craigie and had, of course, sent for Doriennet, giving precise instructions for his journey. Horn had killed the Vallenian, but had been prevented from hiding the body. Freddie's discovery had jeopardised the whole scheme.

With a thorough knowledge of international espionage, Kryn had decided that Kerr and Craigie were the biggest threat. Had he not talked of Kerr when Jules Doriennet had overheard him, the whole thing might have ended differently. He had talked, Kerr had received Doriennet on that warm afternoon when he had planned an afternoon with Lois.

In England, Kryn had put Criff up as the dupe, attracting all eyes and – he had hoped – suspicion on the man who had already played so important a part in international quarrels.

The rest of the English gang had been assembled slowly, kept there for the emergency that might one day break out. Kryn had hoped to pick Kerr off quietly: Doriennet's visit to Kerr had started the tide's turn.

Katrina's idea of changing identities with Rene Mondell had been one of the ugliest facets of the affair, Craigie thought. It had been lucky that Rene had fallen in love with

Falling. Well, Rene was free now: Sir Douglas Mondell had committed suicide when the news had been spread of the real Katrina's death. Von Hauf – the financial wizard of the group – and Horn were to be tried by an international court, sitting *in camera;* there was little doubt as to the issue. Samuel Kingham had followed Mondell's example, and Freddie Kingham would find himself Horn's next of kin.

Odd, thought Freddie afterwards. He would be pretty wealthy. Damn bad business Uncle Matt had been mixed up in that. Made the money stink somehow. That was an idea – he would feel happier if he pushed a lot of the boodle into charity. Feel cleaner. That police woman, Miss Dale, if he could find a girl like that, now!

* * *

Just three weeks after the flight from Baj, Kerr left hospital. He felt oddly deflated, and yet experienced a peculiar happiness. Lois was close to his right side and his left sleeve was empty. They did make decent artificial arms, thank God! But a one-armed man –

Well, it finished him with the Department, and if Lois wanted to change her mind, he would face it.

He said 'if' again when they reached 77g Brook Street, and Lois's answer was more than blunt.

'If you keep on, Bob, you'll have me howling. Do I mind if you've one arm or two, one leg or two? Don't I remember how you lost it? And – it keeps you out of the game, Bob. I don't think I could stand it again. You'll – you'll miss it, but the Burkes were once in the same boat and they – '

Kerr put his right arm about her shoulders. Mold, the perfect servant, coughed discreetly.

'Mr Trale, sir, Mr Oundle and Mr Loftus. And – Lady Mondell, sir.'

Trale had warned Sihilla, but had afterwards been unable to get into Baj because of the rioting. Consequently he had hung around, managed to see a lot and do a little and get a clout over the head. Dodo had been back a week, and had spent a lot of time at Marion's Hospital. What with Carruthers and Davidson – both well on the road to recovery – and Kerr, sick visiting had been the order of the day.

Mold brought in beer, professionally and with tankards.

'Well folk,' said Kerr some minutes later, 'the toast is to the finest bit of acting I've ever seen or heard. *Faita rienta!*'

When the toast had been drunk Rene Mondell looked from Kerr to Lois, and said:

'It's absurd, but I still don't know what it means.'

Kerr chuckled.

'I thought it meant: "it's nothing" once. Apparently it's more literal meaning is: "go and kill yourself". When all's said and done it's lucky Katrina was feared and respected in her palace, but I hope the poor devil didn't go and obey orders. By the way – ' He was still smiling but he spoke more seriously. 'I had a letter from the other Doriennet this morning. He caught a bullet in the chest but he's pulling through.'

There was a moment's silence, and then:

'The toast,' said Bill Loftus quietly, 'is "the Doriennets" – the past and the present.'

THE END

Also now published in Arrow by
John Creasey:

SABOTAGE

A DEPARTMENT Z ADVENTURE

Britain at war, fighting for survival, the population doggedly enduring. Then suddenly, a new threat – an internal one. Vital food stocks are destroyed on a wide scale. Possibly the one threat that could panic the population if it were widely known. And it is. Leaflets are scattered over the country describing in detail what has happened.

Department Z is called in and quickly realise from the scale of the destruction that a big organisation and powerful and highly placed men must be involved. Men who are quite ruthless, who kill openly and without hesitation when they are threatened. Men who use a bizarre variety of agents. Who coldly set their plans in motion behind a smokescreen of confused trails and strange incidents.

REDHEAD

A DEPARTMENT Z ADVENTURE

For the two men the trip to New York had been very successful. Until someone had machine gunned their car and the police had smuggled them out of the country. So they came home. And someone shot at them again. Someone didn't like them. But who? And why? They decided to find out.

At once they were plunged into a search that was to lead them into a series of desperate situations, to involve them in the plans of an American underworld boss to move into Britain, and to end in an amazing pitched battle in the quiet Sussex countryside.